A Second Home

Honoré de Balzac

A Second Home

Copyright © 2024 Indo-European Publishing

The present edition is a reproduction of previous publication of this classic work. Minor typographical errors may have been corrected without note; however, for an authentic reading experience the spelling, punctuation, and capitalization have been retained from the original text.

ISBN: 979-8-88942-364-5

CONTENTS

A SECOND HOME

DEDICATION

To Madame la Comtesse Louise de Turheim as a token of remembrance and affectionate respect.

The Rue du Tourniquet-Saint-Jean, formerly one of the darkest and most tortuous of the streets about the Hotel de Ville, zigzagged round the little gardens of the Paris Prefecture, and ended at the Rue Martroi, exactly at the angle of an old wall now pulled down. Here stood the turnstile to which the street owed its name; it was not removed till 1823, when the Municipality built a ballroom on the garden plot adjoining the Hotel de Ville, for the fete given in honor of the Duc d'Angouleme on his return from Spain.

The widest part of the Rue du Tourniquet was the end opening into the Rue de la Tixeranderie, and even there it was less than six feet across. Hence in rainy weather the gutter water was soon deep at the foot of the old houses, sweeping down with it the dust and refuse deposited at the corner-stones by the residents. As the dust-carts could not pass through, the inhabitants trusted to storms to wash their always miry alley; for how could it be clean? When the summer sun shed its perpendicular rays on Paris like a sheet of gold, but as piercing as the point of a sword, it lighted up the blackness of this street for a few minutes without drying the permanent damp that rose from the ground-floor to the first story of these dark and silent tenements.

The residents, who lighted their lamps at five o'clock in the month of June, in winter never put them out. To this day the enterprising wayfarer who should approach the Marais along the quays, past the end of the Rue du Chaume, the Rues de l'Homme Arme, des Billettes, and des Deux-Portes, all leading to the Rue du Tourniquet, might think he had passed through cellars all the way.

Almost all the streets of old Paris, of which ancient chronicles laud the magnificence, were like this damp and gloomy labyrinth, where the antiquaries still find historical curiosities to admire. For instance, on the house then forming the corner where the Rue du Tourniquet joined the Rue de la Tixeranderie, the clamps might still be seen of two strong iron rings fixed to the wall, the relics of the chains put up every night by the watch to secure public safety.

This house, remarkable for its antiquity, had been constructed in a way that bore witness to the unhealthiness of these old dwellings; for, to preserve the ground-floor from damp, the arches of the cellars rose about two feet above the soil, and the house was entered up three outside steps. The door was crowned by a closed arch, of which the keystone bore a female head and some time-eaten arabesques. Three windows, their sills about five feet from the ground, belonged to a small set of rooms looking out on the Rue du Tourniquet, whence they derived their light. These windows were protected by strong iron bars, very wide apart, and ending below in an outward curve like the bars of a baker's window.

If any passer-by during the day were curious enough to peep into the two rooms forming this little dwelling, he could see nothing; for only under the sun of July could he discern, in the second room, two beds hung with green serge, placed side by side under the paneling of an old-fashioned alcove; but in the afternoon, by about three o'clock, when the candles were lighted, through the pane of the first room an old woman might be seen sitting on a stool by the fireplace, where she nursed the fire in a brazier, to simmer a stew, such as porters' wives are expert in. A few kitchen utensils, hung up against the wall, were visible in the twilight.

At that hour an old table on trestles, but bare of linen, was laid with pewter-spoons, and the dish concocted by the old woman. Three wretched chairs were all the furniture of this room, which was at once the kitchen and the dining-room. Over the chimney-piece were a piece of looking-glass, a tinder-box, three glasses, some matches, and a large, cracked white jug. Still, the floor, the utensils, the fireplace, all gave a pleasant sense of the perfect cleanliness and thrift that pervaded the dull and gloomy home.

The old woman's pale, withered face was quite in harmony with the darkness of the street and the mustiness of the place. As she sat there, motionless, in her chair, it might have been thought that she was as inseparable from the house as a snail from its brown shell; her face, alert with a vague expression of mischief, was framed in a flat cap made of net, which barely covered her white hair; her fine, gray eyes were as quiet as the street, and the many wrinkles in her face might be compared to the cracks in the walls. Whether she had been born to poverty, or had fallen from some past splendor, she now seemed to have been long resigned to her melancholy existence.

From sunrise till dark, excepting when she was getting a meal ready, or, with a basket on her arm, was out purchasing provisions, the old woman sat in the adjoining room by the further window, opposite a young girl. At any hour of the day the passer-by could see the needlewoman seated in an old, red velvet chair, bending over an embroidery frame, and stitching indefatigably.

Her mother had a green pillow on her knee, and busied herself with hand-made net; but her fingers could move the bobbin but slowly; her sight was feeble, for on her nose there rested a pair of those antiquated spectacles which keep their place on the nostrils by the grip of a spring. By night these two hardworking women set a lamp between them; and the light, concentrated by two globe-shaped bottles of water, showed the elder the fine network made by the threads on her pillow, and the younger the most delicate details of the pattern she was embroidering. The outward bend of the window had allowed the girl to rest a box of earth on the window-sill, in which grew some sweet peas, nasturtiums, a sickly little honeysuckle, and some convolvulus that twined its frail stems up the iron bars. These etiolated plants produced a few pale flowers, and added a touch of indescribable sadness and sweetness to the picture offered by this window, in which the two figures were appropriately framed.

The most selfish soul who chanced to see this domestic scene would carry away with him a perfect image of the life led in Paris by the working class of women, for the embroideress evidently lived by her needle. Many, as they passed through the turnstile, found themselves wondering how a girl could preserve her color, living in such a cellar. A student of lively imagination, going that way to cross to the Quartier-Latin, would compare this obscure and vegetative life to that of the ivy that clung to these chill walls, to that of the peasants born to labor, who are born, toil, and die unknown to the world they have helped to feed. A house-owner, after studying the house with the eye of a valuer, would have said, "What will become of those two women if embroidery should go out of fashion?" Among the men who, having some appointment at the Hotel de Ville or the Palais de Justice, were obliged to go through this street at fixed hours, either on their way to business or on their return home, there may have been some charitable soul. Some widower or Adonis of forty, brought so often into the secrets of these sad lives, may perhaps have reckoned on the poverty of this mother and daughter, and have hoped to become the master at no great cost of the innocent work-woman, whose nimble and dimpled fingers, youthful figure, and white skin—a charm due, no doubt, to living in this sunless street—had excited his admiration. Perhaps, again, some honest clerk, with twelve hundred francs a year, seeing every day the diligence the girl gave to her needle, and appreciating the purity of her life, was only waiting for improved prospects to unite one humble life with another, one form of toil to another, and to bring at any rate a man's arm and a calm affection, pale-hued like the flowers in the window, to uphold this home.

Vague hope certainly gave life to the mother's dim, gray eyes. Every morning, after the most frugal breakfast, she took up her pillow, though chiefly for the look of the thing, for she would lay her spectacles on a little mahogany worktable as old as herself, and look out of the window from about half-past eight till ten at the regular passers in the street; she caught their glances, remarked on their gait, their dress, their countenance, and almost seemed to be offering her daughter, her gossiping eyes so evidently tried to attract some magnetic sympathy by manoeuvres worthy of the stage. It was evident that this little review was as good as a play to her, and perhaps her single amusement.

The daughter rarely looked up. Modesty, or a painful consciousness of poverty, seemed to keep her eyes riveted to the work-frame; and only some exclamation of surprise from her mother moved her to show her small features. Then a clerk in a new

5

coat, or who unexpectedly appeared with a woman on his arm, might catch sight of the girl's slightly upturned nose, her rosy mouth, and gray eyes, always bright and lively in spite of her fatiguing toil. Her late hours had left a trace on her face by a pale circle marked under each eye on the fresh rosiness of her cheeks. The poor child looked as if she were made for love and cheerfulness—for love, which had drawn two perfect arches above her eyelids, and had given her such a mass of chestnut hair, that she might have hidden under it as under a tent, impenetrable to the lover's eye—for cheerfulness, which gave quivering animation to her nostrils, which carved two dimples in her rosy cheeks, and made her quick to forget her troubles; cheerfulness, the blossom of hope, which gave her strength to look out without shuddering on the barren path of life.

The girl's hair was always carefully dressed. After the manner of Paris needlewomen, her toilet seemed to her quite complete when she had brushed her hair smooth and tucked up the little short curls that played on each temple in contrast with the whiteness of her skin. The growth of it on the back of her neck was so pretty, and the brown line, so clearly traced, gave such a pleasing idea of her youth and charm, that the observer, seeing her bent over her work, and unmoved by any sound, was inclined to think of her as a coquette. Such inviting promise had excited the interest of more than one young man, who turned round in the vain hope of seeing that modest countenance.

"Caroline, there is a new face that passes regularly by, and not one of the old ones to compare with it."

These words, spoken in a low voice by her mother one August morning in 1815, had vanquished the young needlewoman's indifference, and she looked out on the street; but in vain, the stranger was gone.

"Where has he flown to?" said she.

"He will come back no doubt at four; I shall see him coming, and will touch your foot with mine. I am sure he will come back; he has been through the street regularly for the last three days; but his hours vary. The first day he came by at six o'clock, the day before yesterday it was four, yesterday as early as three. I remember seeing him occasionally some time ago. He is some clerk in the Prefet's office who has moved to the Marais.—Why!" she exclaimed, after glancing down the street, "our gentleman of the brown coat has taken to wearing a wig; how much it alters him!"

The gentleman of the brown coat was, it would seem, the individual who commonly closed the daily procession, for the old woman put on her spectacles and took up her work with a sigh, glancing at her daughter with so strange a look that Lavater himself would have found it difficult to interpret. Admiration, gratitude, a sort of hope for better days, were mingled with pride at having such a pretty daughter.

At about four in the afternoon the old lady pushed her foot against Caroline's, and the girl looked up quickly enough to see the new actor, whose regular advent would thenceforth lend variety to the scene. He was tall and thin, and wore black, a man of about forty, with a certain solemnity of demeanor; as his piercing hazel eye met the old woman's dull gaze, he made her quake, for she felt as though he had the gift of reading hearts, or much practice in it, and his presence must surely be as icy as the air of this dank street. Was the dull, sallow complexion of that ominous face due to excess of work, or the result of delicate health?

The old woman supplied twenty different answers to this question; but Caroline, next day, discerned the lines of long mental suffering on that brow that was so prompt to frown. The rather hollow cheeks of the Unknown bore the stamp of the seal which sorrow sets on its victims as if to grant them the consolation of common recognition and brotherly union for resistance. Though the girl's expression was at first one of lively but innocent curiosity, it assumed a look of gentle sympathy as the stranger receded from view, like a last relation following in a funeral train.

The heat of the weather was so great, and the gentleman was so absent-minded, that he had taken off his hat and forgotten to put it on again as he went down the squalid street. Caroline could see the stern look given to his countenance by the way the hair was brushed from his forehead. The strong impression, devoid of charm, made on the girl by this man's appearance was totally unlike any sensation produced by the other passengers who used the street; for the first time in her life she was moved to pity for some one else than herself and her mother; she made no reply to the absurd conjectures that supplied material for the old woman's provoking volubility, and drew her long needle in silence through the web of stretched net; she only regretted not having seen the stranger more closely, and looked forward to the morrow to form a definite opinion of him.

It was the first time, indeed, that a man passing down the street had ever given rise to much thought in her mind. She generally had nothing but a smile in response to her mother's hypotheses, for the old woman looked on every passer-by as a possible protector for her daughter. And if such suggestions, so crudely presented, gave rise to no evil thoughts in Caroline's mind, her indifference must be ascribed to the persistent and unfortunately inevitable toil in which the energies of her sweet youth were being spent, and which would infallibly mar the clearness of her eyes or steal from her fresh cheeks the bloom that still colored them.

For two months or more the "Black Gentleman"—the name they had given him—was erratic in his movements; he did not always come down the Rue du Tourniquet; the old woman sometimes saw him in the evening when he had not passed in the morning, and he did not come by at such regular hours as the clerks who served Madame Crochard instead of a clock; moreover, excepting on the first occasion, when his look had given the old mother a sense of alarm, his eyes had never once dwelt on the weird picture of these two female gnomes. With the exception of two carriage-gates and a dark ironmonger's shop, there were in the Rue du Tourniquet only barred windows, giving light to the staircases of the neighboring houses; thus the stranger's lack of curiosity was not to be accounted for by the presence of dangerous rivals; and Madame Crochard was greatly piqued to see her "Black Gentleman" always lost in thought, his eyes fixed on the ground, or straight before him, as though he hoped to read the future in the fog of the Rue du Tourniquet. However, one morning, about the middle of September, Caroline Crochard's roguish face stood out so brightly against the dark background of the room, looking so fresh among the belated flowers and faded leaves that twined round the window-bars, the daily scene was gay with such contrasts of light and shade, of pink and white blending with the light material on which the pretty needlewoman was working, and with the red and brown hues of the chairs, that the stranger gazed very attentively at the effects of this living picture. In point of fact, the old woman, provoked by her "Black Gentleman's" indifference, had made such a clatter with her bobbins that the gloomy and pensive passer-by was perhaps prompted to look up by the unusual noise.

The stranger merely exchanged glances with Caroline, swift indeed, but enough to effect a certain contact between their souls, and both were aware that they would think of each other. When the stranger came by again, at four in the afternoon, Caroline recognized the sound of his step on the echoing pavement; they looked steadily at each other, and with evident purpose; his eyes had an expression of kindliness which made him smile, and Caroline colored; the old mother noted them with satisfaction. Ever after that memorable afternoon, the Gentleman in Black went by twice a day, with rare exceptions, which both the women observed. They concluded from the irregularity of the hours of his homecoming that he was not released so early, nor so precisely punctual as a subordinate official.

All through the first three winter months, twice a day, Caroline and the stranger thus saw each other for so long as it took him to traverse the piece of road that lay along the length of the door and three windows of the house. Day after day this brief interview had the hue of friendly sympathy which at last had acquired a sort of fraternal kindness. Caroline and the stranger seemed to understand each other from the first; and then, by dint of scrutinizing each other's faces, they learned to know them well. Ere long it came to be, as it were, a visit that the Unknown owed to Caroline; if by any chance her Gentleman in Black went by without bestowing on her the half-smile of his expressive lips, or the cordial glance of his brown eyes, something was missing to her all day. She felt as an old man does to whom the daily study of a newspaper is such an indispensable pleasure that on the day after any great holiday he wanders about quite lost, and seeking, as much out of vagueness as for want of patience, the sheet by which he cheats an hour of life.

But these brief meetings had the charm of intimate friendliness, quite as much for the stranger as for Caroline. The girl could no more hide a vexation, a grief, or some slight ailment from the keen eye of her appreciative friend than he could conceal anxiety from hers.

"He must have had some trouble yesterday," was the thought that constantly arose in the embroideress' mind as she saw some change in the features of the "Black Gentleman."

"Oh, he has been working too hard!" was a reflection due to another shade of expression which Caroline could discern.

The stranger, on his part, could guess when the girl had spent Sunday in finishing a dress, and he felt an interest in the pattern. As quarter-day came near he could see that her pretty face was clouded by anxiety, and he could guess when Caroline had sat up late at work; but above all, he noted how the gloomy thoughts that dimmed the cheerful and delicate features of her young face gradually vanished by degrees as their acquaintance ripened. When winter had killed the climbers and plants of her window garden, and the window was kept closed, it was not without a smile of gentle amusement that the stranger observed the concentration of the light within, just at the level of Caroline's head. The very small fire and the frosty red of the two women's faces betrayed the poverty of their home; but if ever his own countenance expressed regretful compassion, the girl proudly met it with assumed cheerfulness.

Meanwhile the feelings that had arisen in their hearts remained buried there, no incident occurring to reveal to either of them how deep and strong they were in the other; they had never even heard the sound of each other's voice. These mute friends were even on their guard against any nearer acquaintance, as though it meant disaster. Each seemed to fear lest it should bring on the other some grief more serious than those they felt tempted to share. Was it shyness or friendship that checked them? Was it a dread of meeting with selfishness, or the odious distrust which sunders all the residents within the walls of a populous city? Did the voice of conscience warn them of approaching danger? It would be impossible to explain the instinct which made them as much enemies as friends, at once indifferent and attached, drawn to each other by impulse, and severed by circumstance. Each perhaps hoped to preserve a cherished illusion. It might almost have been thought that the stranger feared lest he should hear some vulgar word from those lips as fresh and pure as a flower, and that Caroline felt herself unworthy of the mysterious personage who was evidently possessed of power and wealth.

As to Madame Crochard, that tender mother, almost angry at her daughter's persistent lack of decisiveness, now showed a sulky face to the "Black Gentleman," on whom she had hitherto smiled with a sort of benevolent servility. Never before had she complained so bitterly of being compelled, at her age, to do the cooking; never had her catarrh and her rheumatism wrung so many groans from her; finally, she could not, this winter, promise so many ells of net as Caroline had hitherto been able to count on.

Under these circumstances, and towards the end of December, at the time when bread was dearest, and that dearth of corn was beginning to be felt which made the year 1816 so hard on the poor, the stranger observed on the features of the girl whose name was still unknown to him, the painful traces of a secret sorrow which his kindest smiles could not dispel. Before long he saw in Caroline's eyes the dimness attributed to long hours at night. One night, towards the end of the month, the Gentleman in Black passed down the Rue du Tourniquet at the quite unwonted hour of one in the morning. The perfect silence allowed of his hearing before passing the house the lachrymose voice of the old mother, and Caroline's even sadder tones, mingling with the swish of a shower of sleet. He crept along as slowly as he could; and then, at the risk of being taken up by the police, he stood still below the window to hear the mother and daughter, while watching them through the largest of the holes in the yellow muslin curtains, which were eaten away by wear as a cabbage leaf is riddled by caterpillars. The inquisitive stranger saw a sheet of paper on the table that stood between the two work-frames, and on which stood the lamp and the globes filled with water. He at once identified it as a writ. Madame Crochard was weeping, and Caroline's voice was thick, and had lost its sweet, caressing tone.

"Why be so heartbroken, mother? Monsieur Molineux will not sell us up or turn us out before I have finished this dress; only two nights more and I shall take it home to Madame Roguin."

"And supposing she keeps you waiting as usual?—And will the money for the gown pay the baker too?"

The spectator of this scene had long practice in reading faces; he fancied he could discern that the mother's grief was as false as the daughter's was genuine; he turned away, and presently came back. When he next peeped through the hole in the curtain, Madame Crochard was in bed. The young needlewoman, bending over her frame, was embroidering with indefatigable diligence; on the table, with the writ lay a triangular hunch of bread, placed there, no doubt, to sustain her in the night and to remind her of the reward of her industry. The stranger was tremulous with pity and sympathy; he threw his purse in through a cracked pane so that it should fall at the girl's feet; and then, without waiting to enjoy her surprise, he escaped, his cheeks tingling.

Next morning the shy and melancholy stranger went past with a look of deep preoccupation, but he could not escape Caroline's gratitude; she had opened her window and affected to be digging in the square window-box buried in snow, a pretext of which the clumsy ingenuity plainly told her benefactor that she had been resolved not to see him only through the pane. Her eyes were full of tears as she bowed her head, as much as to say to her benefactor, "I can only repay you from my heart."

But the Gentleman in Black affected not to understand the meaning of this sincere gratitude. In the evening, as he came by, Caroline was busy mending the window with a sheet of paper, and she smiled at him, showing her row of pearly teeth like a promise. Thenceforth the Stranger went another way, and was no more seen in the Rue due Tourniquet.

It was one day early in the following May that, as Caroline was giving the roots of the honeysuckle a glass of water, one Saturday morning, she caught sight of a narrow strip of cloudless blue between the black lines of houses, and said to her mother:

"Mamma, we must go to-morrow for a trip to Montmorency!"

She had scarcely uttered the words, in a tone of glee, when the Gentleman in Black came by, sadder and more dejected than ever. Caroline's innocent and ingratiating glance might have been taken for an invitation. And, in fact, on the following day, when Madame Crochard, dressed in a pelisse of claret-colored merinos, a silk bonnet, and striped shawl of an imitation Indian pattern, came out to choose seats in a chaise at the corner of the Rue du Faubourg Saint-Denis and the Rue d'Enghien, there she found her Unknown standing like a man waiting for his wife. A smile of pleasure lighted up the Stranger's face when his eye fell on Caroline, her neat feet shod in plum-colored prunella gaiters, and her white dress tossed by a breeze that would have been fatal to an ill-made woman, but which displayed her graceful form. Her face, shaded by a rice-straw bonnet lined with pink silk, seemed to beam with a reflection from heaven; her broad, plum-colored belt set off a waist he could have spanned; her hair, parted in two brown bands over a forehead as white as snow, gave her an expression of innocence which no other feature contradicted. Enjoyment seemed to have made Caroline as light as the straw of her hat; but when she saw the Gentleman in Black, radiant hope suddenly eclipsed her bright dress and her beauty. The Stranger, who appeared to be in doubt, had not perhaps made up his mind to be the girl's escort for the day till this revelation of the delight she felt on seeing him. He at once hired a vehicle with a fairly good horse, to drive to Saint-Leu-Taverny, and he offered Madame Crochard and her daughter seats by his side. The mother accepted without ado; but presently, when they were already on the way to Saint-Denis, she was by way of having scruples, and made a few civil speeches as to the possible inconvenience two women might cause their companion.

"Perhaps, monsieur, you wished to drive alone to Saint-Leu-Taverny," said she, with affected simplicity.

Before long she complained of the heat, and especially of her cough, which, she said, had hindered her from closing her eyes all night; and by the time the carriage had reached Saint-Denis, Madame Crochard seemed to be fast asleep. Her snores, indeed, seemed, to the Gentleman in Black, rather doubtfully genuine, and he frowned as he looked at the old woman with a very suspicious eye.

"Oh, she is fast asleep," said Caroline quilelessly; "she never ceased coughing all night. She must be very tired."

Her companion made no reply, but he looked at the girl with a smile that seemed to say:

"Poor child, you little know your mother!"

However, in spite of his distrust, as the chaise made its way down the long avenue of poplars leading to Eaubonne, the Stranger thought that Madame Crochard was really asleep; perhaps he did not care to inquire how far her slumbers were genuine or feigned.

Whether it were that the brilliant sky, the pure country air, and the heady fragrance of the first green shoots of the poplars, the catkins of willow, and the flowers of the blackthorn had inclined his heart to open like all the nature around him; or that any long restraint was too oppressive while Caroline's sparkling eyes responded to his own, the Gentleman in Black entered on a conversation with his young companion, as aimless as the swaying of the branches in the wind, as devious as the flitting of the butterflies in the azure air, as illogical as the melodious murmur of the fields, and, like it, full of mysterious love. At that season is not the rural country as tremulous as a bride that has donned her marriage robe; does it not invite the coldest soul to be happy? What heart could remain unthawed, and what lips could keep its secret, on leaving the gloomy streets of the Marais for the first time since the previous autumn, and entering the smiling and picturesque valley of Montmorency; on seeing it in the morning light, its endless horizons receding from view; and then lifting a charmed gaze to eyes which expressed no less infinitude mingled with love?

The Stranger discovered that Caroline was sprightly rather than witty, affectionate, but ill educated; but while her laugh was giddy, her words promised genuine feeling. When, in response to her companion's shrewd questioning, the girl spoke with the heartfelt effusiveness of which the lower classes are lavish, not guarding it with reticence like people of the world, the Black Gentleman's face brightened, and seemed to renew its youth. His countenance by degrees lost the sadness that lent sternness to his features, and little by little they gained a look of handsome youthfulness which made Caroline proud and happy. The pretty needlewoman guessed that her new friend had been long weaned from tenderness and love, and no longer believed in the devotion of woman. Finally, some unexpected sally in Caroline's light prattle lifted the last veil that concealed the real youth and genuine character of the Stranger's physiognomy; he seemed to bid farewell to the ideas that haunted him, and showed the natural liveliness that lay beneath the solemnity of his expression.

Their conversation had insensibly become so intimate, that by the time when the carriage stopped at the first houses of the straggling village of Saint-Leu, Caroline was calling the gentleman Monsieur Roger. Then for the first time the old mother awoke.

"Caroline, she has heard everything!" said Roger suspiciously in the girl's ear.

Caroline's reply was an exquisite smile of disbelief, which dissipated the dark cloud that his fear of some plot on the old woman's part had brought to this suspicious mortal's brow. Madame Crochard was amazed at nothing, approved of everything, followed her daughter and Monsieur Roger into the park, where the two young people had agreed to wander through the smiling meadows and fragrant copses made famous by the taste of Queen Hortense.

"Good heavens! how lovely!" exclaimed Caroline when standing on the green ridge where the forest of Montmorency begins, she saw lying at her feet the wide valley with its combes sheltering scattered villages, its horizon of blue hills, its church towers, its meadows and fields, whence a murmur came up, to die on her ear like the swell of the ocean. The three wanderers made their way by the bank of an artificial stream and came to the Swiss valley, where stands a chalet that had more than once given shelter to Hortense and Napoleon. When Caroline had seated herself with pious reverence on the mossy wooden bench where kings and princesses and the Emperor had rested, Madame Crochard expressed a wish to have a nearer view of a bridge that hung across between two rocks at some little distance, and bent her steps towards that rural curiosity, leaving her daughter in Monsieur Roger's care, though telling them that she would not go out of sight.

"What, poor child!" cried Roger, "have you never longed for wealth and the pleasures of luxury? Have you never wished that you might wear the beautiful dresses you embroider?"

"It would not be the truth, Monsieur Roger, if I were to tell you that I never think how happy people must be who are rich. Oh yes! I often fancy, especially when I am going to sleep, how glad I should be to see my poor mother no longer compelled to go out, whatever the weather, to buy our little provisions, at her age. I should like her to have a servant who, every morning before she was up, would bring her up her coffee, nicely sweetened with white sugar. And she loves reading novels, poor dear soul! Well, and I would rather see her wearing out her eyes over her favorite books than over twisting her bobbins from morning till night. And again, she ought to have a little good wine. In short, I should like to see her comfortable—she is so good."

"Then she has shown you great kindness?"

"Oh yes," said the girl, in a tone of conviction. Then, after a short pause, during which the two young people stood watching Madame Crochard, who had got to the middle of the rustic bridge, and was shaking her finger at them, Caroline went on:

"Oh yes, she has been so good to me. What care she took of me when I was little! She sold her last silver forks to apprentice me to the old maid who taught me to embroider.—And my poor father! What did she not go through to make him end his days in happiness!" The girl shivered at the remembrance, and hid her face in her hands.—"Well! come! let us forget past sorrows!" she added, trying to rally her high spirits. She blushed as she saw that Roger too was moved, but she dared not look at him.

"What was your father?" he asked.

"He was an opera-dancer before the Revolution," said she, with an air of perfect simplicity, "and my mother sang in the chorus. My father, who was leader of the figures on the stage, happened to be present at the siege of the Bastille. He was recognized by some of the assailants, who asked him whether he could not lead a real attack, since he was used to leading such enterprises on the boards. My father was brave; he accepted the post, led the insurgents, and was rewarded by the nomination to the rank of captain in the army of Sambre-et-Meuse, where he distinguished himself so far as to rise rapidly to be a colonel. But at Lutzen he was so badly wounded that, after a year's sufferings, he died in Paris. — The Bourbons returned; my mother could obtain no pension, and we fell into such abject misery that we were compelled to work for our living. For some time past she has been ailing, poor dear, and I have never known her so little resigned; she complains a good deal, and, indeed, I cannot wonder, for she has known the pleasures of an easy life. For my part, I cannot pine for delights I have never known, I have but one thing to wish for."

"And that is?" said Roger eagerly, as if roused from a dream.

"That women may continue to wear embroidered net dresses, so that I may never lack work."

The frankness of this confession interested the young man, who looked with less hostile eyes on Madame Crochard as she slowly made her way back to them.

"Well, children, have you had a long talk?" said she, with a half-laughing, half-indulgent air. "When I think, Monsieur Roger, that the 'little Corporal' has sat where you are sitting," she went on after a pause. "Poor man! how my husband worshiped him! Ah! Crochard did well to die, for he could not have borne to think of him where they have sent him!"

Roger put his finger to his lips, and the good woman went on very gravely, with a shake of her head:

"All right, mouth shut and tongue still! But," added she, unhooking a bit of her bodice, and showing a ribbon and cross tied round her neck by a piece of black ribbon, "they shall never hinder me from wearing what he gave to my poor Crochard, and I will have it buried with me."

On hearing this speech, which at that time was regarded as

seditious, Roger interrupted the old lady by rising suddenly, and they returned to the village through the park walks. The young man left them for a few minutes while he went to order a meal at the best eating-house in Taverny; then, returning to fetch them, he led the way through the alleys cut in the forest.

The dinner was cheerful. Roger was no longer the melancholy shade that was wont to pass along the Rue du Tourniquet; he was not the "Black Gentleman," but rather a confiding young man ready to take life as it came, like the two hard-working women who, on the morrow, might lack bread; he seemed alive to all the joys of youth, his smile was quite affectionate and childlike.

When, at five o'clock, this happy meal was ended with a few glasses of champagne, Roger was the first to propose that they should join the village ball under the chestnuts, where he and Caroline danced together. Their hands met with sympathetic pressure, their hearts beat with the same hopes; and under the blue sky and the slanting, rosy beams of sunset, their eyes sparkled with fires which, to them, made the glory of the heavens pale. How strange is the power of an idea, of a desire! To these two nothing seemed impossible. In such magic moments, when enjoyment sheds its reflections on the future, the soul foresees nothing but happiness. This sweet day had created memories for these two to which nothing could be compared in all their past existence. Would the source prove to be more beautiful than the river, the desire more enchanting than its gratification, the thing hoped for more delightful than the thing possessed?

"So the day is already at an end!" On hearing this exclamation from her unknown friend when the dance was over, Caroline looked at him compassionately, as his face assumed once more a faint shade of sadness.

"Why should you not be as happy in Paris as you are here?" she asked. "Is happiness to be found only at Saint-Leu? It seems to me that I can henceforth never be unhappy anywhere."

Roger was struck by these words, spoken with the glad unrestraint that always carries a woman further than she intended, just as prudery often lends her greater cruelty than she feels. For the first time since that glance, which had, in a way, been the beginning of their friendship, Caroline and Roger had the same idea; though they did not express it, they felt it at the same instant, as a result of a common impression like that of a comforting fire cheering both under the frost of winter; then, as if frightened by each other's silence, they made their way to the spot where the carriage was waiting. But before getting into it, they playfully took hands and ran together down the dark avenue in front of Madame Crochard. When they could no longer see the white net cap, which showed as a speck through the leaves where the old woman was—"Caroline!" said Roger in a tremulous voice, and with a beating heart.

The girl was startled, and drew back a few steps, understanding the invitation this question conveyed; however, she held out her hand, which was passionately kissed, but which she hastily withdrew, for by standing on tiptoe she could see her mother.

Madame Crochard affected blindness, as if, with a reminiscence of her old parts, she was only required to figure as a supernumerary.

The adventures of these two young people were not continued in the Rue du Tourniquet. To see Roger and Caroline once more, we must leap into the heart of modern Paris, where, in some of the newly-built houses, there are apartments that seem made on purpose for newly-married couples to spend their honeymoon in. There the paper and paint are as fresh as the bride and bridegroom, and the decorations are in blossom like their love; everything is in harmony with youthful notions and ardent wishes.

Half-way down the Rue Taitbout, in a house whose stone walls were still white, where the columns of the hall and the doorway were as yet spotless, and the inner walls shone with the neat painting which our recent intimacy with English ways had brought into fashion, there was, on the second floor, a small set of rooms fitted by the architect as though he had known what their use would be. A simple airy ante-room, with a stucco dado, formed an entrance into a drawing-room and dining-room. Out of the drawing-room opened a pretty bedroom, with a bathroom beyond. Every chimney-shelf had over it a fine mirror elegantly framed. The doors were crowded with arabesques in good taste, and the cornices were in the best style. Any amateur would have discerned there the sense of distinction and decorative fitness which mark the work of modern French architects.

For above a month Caroline had been at home in this apartment, furnished by an upholsterer who submitted to an artist's guidance. A short description of the principal room will suffice to give us an idea of the wonders it offered to Caroline's delighted eyes when Roger installed her there. Hangings of gray stuff trimmed with green silk adorned the walls of her bedroom; the seats, covered with light-colored woolen sateen, were of easy and comfortable shapes, and in the latest fashion; a chest of drawers of some simple wood, inlaid with lines of a darker hue, contained the treasures of the toilet; a writing-table to match served for inditing love-letters on scented paper; the bed, with antique draperies, could not fail to suggest thoughts of love by its soft hangings of elegant muslin; the window-curtains, of drab silk with green fringe, were always half drawn to subdue the light; a bronze clock represented Love crowning Psyche; and a carpet of Gothic design on a red ground set off the other accessories of this delightful retreat. There was a small dressing-table in front of a long glass, and here the needlewoman sat, out of patience with Plaisir, the famous hairdresser.

"Do you think you will have done to-day?" said she.

"Your hair is so long and so thick, madame," replied Plaisir.

Caroline could not help smiling. The man's flattery had no doubt revived in her mind the memory of the passionate praises lavished by her lover on the beauty of her hair, which he delighted in.

The hairdresser having done, a waiting-maid came and held counsel with her as to the dress in which Roger would like best to see her. It was the beginning of September 1816, and the weather was cold; she chose a green grenadine trimmed with chinchilla. As soon as she was dressed, Caroline flew into the drawing-room and opened a window, out of which she stepped on to the elegant balcony, that adorned the front of the house; there she stood, with her arms crossed, in a charming attitude, not to show herself to the admiration of the passers-by and see them turn to gaze at her, but to be able to look out on the Boulevard at the bottom of the Rue Taitbout. This side view, really very comparable to the peephole made by actors in the drop-scene of a theatre, enabled her to catch a glimpse of numbers of elegant carriages, and a crowd of persons, swept past with the rapidity of Ombres Chinoises. Not knowing whether Roger would arrive in a carriage or on foot, the needlewoman from the Rue du Tourniquet looked by turns at the foot-passengers, and at the tilburies—light cabs introduced into Paris by the English.

Expressions of refractoriness and of love passed by turns over her youthful face when, after waiting for a quarter of an hour, neither her keen eye nor her heart had announced the arrival of him whom she knew to be due. What disdain, what indifference were shown in her beautiful features for all the other creatures who were bustling like ants below her feet. Her gray eyes, sparkling with fun, now positively flamed. Given over to her passion, she avoided admiration with as much care as the proudest devote to encouraging it when they drive about Paris, certainly feeling no care as to whether her fair countenance leaning over the balcony, or her little foot between the bars, and the picture of her bright eyes and delicious turned-up nose would be effaced or no from the minds of the passers-by who admired them; she saw but one face, and had but one idea. When the spotted head of a certain bay horse happened to cross the narrow strip between the two rows of houses, Caroline gave a little shiver and stood on tiptoe in hope of recognizing the white traces and the color of the tilbury. It was he!

Roger turned the corner of the street, saw the balcony, whipped the horse, which came up at a gallop, and stopped at the bronze-green door that he knew as well as his master did. The door of the apartment was opened at once by the maid, who had heard her mistress' exclamation of delight. Roger rushed up to the drawing-room, clasped Caroline in his arms, and embraced her with the effusive feeling natural when two beings who love each other rarely meet. He led her, or rather they went by a common impulse, their arms about each other, into the quiet and fragrant bedroom; a settee stood ready for them to sit by the fire, and for a moment they looked at each other in silence, expressing their happiness only by their clasped hands, and communicating their thoughts in a fond gaze.

"Yes, it is he!" she said at last. "Yes, it is you. Do you know, I have not seen you for three long days, an age!—But what is the matter? You are unhappy."

"My poor Caroline—"

"There, you see! 'poor Caroline'—"

"No, no, do not laugh, my darling; we cannot go to the Feydeau Theatre together this evening."

Caroline put on a little pout, but it vanished immediately.

"How absurd I am! How can I think of going to the play when I see you? Is not the sight of you the only spectacle I care for?" she cried, pushing her fingers through Roger's hair.

"I am obliged to go to the Attorney-General's. We have a knotty case in hand. He met me in the great hall at the Palais; and as I am to plead, he asked me to dine with him. But, my dearest, you can go to the theatre with your mother, and I will join you if the meeting breaks up early."

"To the theatre without you!" cried she in a tone of amazement; "enjoy any pleasure you do not share! O my Roger! you do not deserve a kiss," she added, throwing her arms round his neck with an artless and impassioned impulse.

"Caroline, I must go home and dress. The Marais is some way off, and I still have some business to finish."

"Take care what you are saying, monsieur," said she, interrupting him. "My mother says that when a man begins to talk about his business, he is ceasing to love."

"Caroline! Am I not here? Have I not stolen this hour from my pitiless—"

"Hush!" said she, laying a finger on his mouth. "Don't you see that I am in jest."

They had now come back to the drawing-room, and Roger's eye fell on an object brought home that morning by the cabinetmaker. Caroline's old rosewood embroidery-frame, by which she and her mother had earned their bread when they lived in the Rue du Tourniquet-Saint-Jean, had been refitted and polished, and a net dress, of elaborate design, was already stretched upon it.

"Well, then, my dear, I shall do some work this evening. As I stitch, I shall fancy myself gone back to those early days when you used to pass by me without a word, but not without a glance; the days when the remembrance of your look kept me awake all night. Oh my dear old frame—the best piece of furniture in my room, though you did not give it me!—You cannot think," said she, seating herself on Roger's knees; for he, overcome by irresistible feelings, had dropped into a chair. "Listen.—All I can earn by my work I mean to give to the poor. You have made me rich. How I love that pretty home at Bellefeuille, less because of what it is than because you gave it me! But tell me, Roger, I should like to call myself Caroline de Bellefeuille—can I? You must know: is it legal or permissible?"

As she saw a little affirmative grimace—for Roger hated the name of Crochard—Caroline jumped for glee, and clapped her hands.

"I feel," said she, "as if I should more especially belong to you. Usually a woman gives up her own name and takes her husband's—" An idea forced itself upon her and made her blush. She took Roger's hand and led him to the open piano.—"Listen," said she, "I can play my sonata now like an angel!" and her fingers were already running over the ivory keys, when she felt herself seized round the waist.

"Caroline, I ought to be far from hence!"

"You insist on going? Well, go," said she, with a pretty pout, but she smiled as she looked at the clock and exclaimed joyfully, "At any rate, I have detained you a quarter of an hour!"

"Good-bye, Mademoiselle de Bellefeuille," said he, with the gentle irony of love.

She kissed him and saw her lover to the door; when the sound of his steps had died away on the stairs she ran out on to the balcony to see him get into the tilbury, to see him gather up the reins, to catch a parting look, hear the crack of his whip and the sound of his wheels on the stones, watch the handsome horse, the master's hat, the tiger's gold lace, and at last to stand gazing long after the dark corner of the street had eclipsed this vision.

Five years after Mademoiselle Caroline de Bellefeuille had taken up her abode in the pretty house in the Rue Taitbout, we again look in on one of those home-scenes which tighten the bonds of affection between two persons who truly love. In the middle of the blue drawing-room, in front of the window opening to the balcony, a little boy of four was making a tremendous noise as he whipped the rocking-horse, whose two curved supports for the legs did not move fast enough to please him; his pretty face, framed in fair curls that fell over his white collar, smiled up like a cherub's at his mother when she said to him from the depths of an easy-chair, "Not so much noise, Charles; you will wake your little sister."

The inquisitive boy suddenly got off his horse, and treading on tiptoe as if he were afraid of the sound of his feet on the carpet, came up with one finger between his little teeth, and standing in one of those childish attitudes that are so graceful because they are so perfectly natural, raised the muslin veil that hid the rosy face of a little girl sleeping on her mother's knee.

"Is Eugenie asleep, then?" said he, quite astonished. "Why is she asleep when we are awake?" he added, looking up with large, liquid black eyes.

"That only God can know," replied Caroline, with a smile.

The mother and boy gazed at the infant, only that morning baptized.

Caroline, now about four-and-twenty, showed the ripe beauty which had expanded under the influence of cloudless happiness and constant enjoyment. In her the Woman was complete.

Delighted to obey her dear Roger's every wish, she had acquired the accomplishments she had lacked; she played the piano fairly well, and sang sweetly. Ignorant of the customs of a world that would have treated her as an outcast, and which she would not have cared for even if it had welcomed her—for a happy woman does not care for the world—she had not caught the elegance of manner or learned the art of conversation, abounding in words and devoid of ideas, which is current in fashionable drawing-rooms; on the other hand, she worked hard to gain the knowledge indispensable to a mother whose chief ambition is to bring up her children well. Never to lose sight of her boy, to give him from the cradle that training of every minute which impresses on the young a love of all that is good and beautiful, to shelter him from every evil influence and fulfil both the painful duties of a nurse and the tender offices of a mother,—these were her chief pleasures.

The coy and gentle being had from the first day so fully resigned herself never to step beyond the enchanted sphere where she found all her happiness, that, after six years of the tenderest intimacy, she still knew her lover only by the name of Roger. A print of the picture of the Psyche lighting her lamp to gaze on Love in spite of his prohibition, hung in her room, and constantly reminded her of the conditions of her happiness. Through all these six years her humble pleasures had never importuned Roger by a single indiscreet ambition, and his heart was a treasure-house of kindness. Never had she longed for diamonds or fine clothes, and had again and again refused the luxury of a carriage which he had offered her. To look out from her balcony for Roger's cab, to go with him to the play or make excursions with him, on fine days in the environs of Paris, to long for him, to see him, and then to long again,—these made up the history of her life, poor in incidents but rich in happiness.

As she rocked the infant, now a few months old, on her knee, singing the while, she allowed herself to recall the memories of the past. She lingered more especially on the months of September, when Roger was accustomed to take her to Bellefeuille and spend the delightful days which seem to combine the charms of every season. Nature is equally prodigal of flowers and fruit, the evenings are mild, the mornings bright, and a blaze of summer often returns after a spell of autumn gloom. During the early days of their love, Caroline had ascribed the even mind and gentle temper, of which Roger gave her so many proofs, to the rarity of their always longed-for meetings, and to their mode of life, which did not compel them to be constantly together, as a husband and wife must be. But now she could remember with rapture that, tortured by foolish fears, she had watched him with trembling during their first stay on this little estate in the Gatinais. Vain suspiciousness of love! Each of these months of happiness had passed like a dream in the midst of joys which never rang false. She had always seen that kind creature with a tender smile on his lips, a smile that seemed to mirror her own.

As she called up these vivid pictures, her eyes filled with tears;

she thought she could not love him enough, and was tempted to regard her ambiguous position as a sort of tax levied by Fate on her love. Finally, invincible curiosity led her to wonder for the thousandth time what events they could be that led so tender a heart as Roger's to find his pleasure in clandestine and illicit happiness. She invented a thousand romances on purpose really to avoid recognizing the true reason, which she had long suspected but tried not to believe in. She rose, and carrying the baby in her arms, went into the dining-room to superintend the preparations for dinner.

It was the 6th of May 1822, the anniversary of the excursion to the Park of Saint-Leu, which had been the turning-point of her life; each year it had been marked by heartfelt rejoicing. Caroline chose the linen to be used, and arranged the dessert. Having attended with joy to these details, which touched Roger, she placed the infant in her pretty cot and went out on to the balcony, whence she presently saw the carriage which her friend, as he grew to riper years, now used instead of the smart tilbury of his youth. After submitting to the first fire of Caroline's embraces and the kisses of the little rogue who addressed him as papa, Roger went to the cradle, looked at his little sleeping daughter, kissed her forehead, and then took out of his pocket a document covered with black writing.

"Caroline," said he, "here is the marriage portion of Mademoiselle Eugenie de Bellefeuille."

The mother gratefully took the paper, a deed of gift of securities in the State funds.

"Buy why," said she, "have you given Eugenie three thousand francs a year, and Charles no more than fifteen hundred?"

"Charles, my love, will be a man," replied he. "Fifteen hundred francs are enough for him. With so much for certain, a man of courage is above poverty. And if by chance your son should turn out a nonentity, I do not wish him to be able to play the fool. If he is

ambitious, this small income will give him a taste for work.—
Eugenie is a girl; she must have a little fortune."

The father then turned to play with his boy, whose effusive
affection showed the independence and freedom in which he was
brought up. No sort of shyness between the father and child
interfered with the charm which rewards a parent for his devotion;
and the cheerfulness of the little family was as sweet as it was
genuine. In the evening a magic-lantern displayed its illusions and
mysterious pictures on a white sheet to Charles' great surprise, and
more than once the innocent child's heavenly rapture made
Caroline and Roger laugh heartily.

Later, when the little boy was in bed, the baby woke and
craved its limpid nourishment. By the light of a lamp in the
chimney corner, Roger enjoyed the scene of peace and comfort, and
gave himself up to the happiness of contemplating the sweet
picture of the child clinging to Caroline's white bosom as she sat, as
fresh as a newly opened lily, while her hair fell in long brown curls
that almost hid her neck. The lamplight enhanced the grace of the
young mother, shedding over her, her dress, and the infant, the
picturesque effects of strong light and shadow.

The calm and silent woman's face struck Roger as a thousand
times sweeter than ever, and he gazed tenderly at the rosy, pouting
lips from which no harsh word had ever been heard. The very same
thought was legible in Caroline's eyes as she gave a sidelong look at
Roger, either to enjoy the effect she was producing on him, or to see
what the end of the evening was to be. He, understanding the
meaning of this cunning glance, said with assumed regret, "I must
be going. I have a serious case to be finished, and I am expected at
home. Duty before all things—don't you think so, my darling?"

Caroline looked him in the face with an expression at once sad
and sweet, with the resignation which does not, however, disguise
the pangs of a sacrifice.

"Good-bye, then," said she. "Go, for if you stay an hour longer
I cannot so lightly bear to set you free."

"My dearest," said he with a smile, "I have three days' holiday, and am supposed to be twenty leagues away from Paris."

A few days after this anniversary of the 6th of May, Mademoiselle de Bellefeuille hurried off one morning to the Rue Saint-Louis, in the Marais, only hoping she might not arrive too late at a house where she commonly went once a week. An express messenger had just come to inform her that her mother, Madame Crochard, was sinking under a complication of disorders produced by constant catarrh and rheumatism.

While the hackney coach-driver was flogging up his horses at Caroline's urgent request, supported by the promise of a handsome present, the timid old women, who had been Madame Crochard's friends during her later years, had brought a priest into the neat and comfortable second-floor rooms occupied by the old widow. Madame Crochard's maid did not know that the pretty lady at whose house her mistress so often dined was her daughter, and she was one of the first to suggest the services of a confessor, in the hope that this priest might be at least as useful to herself as to the sick woman. Between two games of boston, or out walking in the Jardin Turc, the old beldames with whom the widow gossiped all day had succeeded in rousing in their friend's stony heart some scruples as to her former life, some visions of the future, some fears of hell, and some hopes of forgiveness if she should return in sincerity to a religious life. So on this solemn morning three ancient females had settled themselves in the drawing-room where Madame Crochard was "at home" every Tuesday. Each in turn left her armchair to go to the poor old woman's bedside and sit with her, giving her the false hopes with which people delude the dying.

At the same time, when the end was drawing near, when the physician called in the day before would no longer answer for her life, the three dames took counsel together as to whether it would not be well to send word to Mademoiselle de Bellefeuille. Francoise having been duly informed, it was decided that a commissionaire should go to the Rue Taitbout to inform the young relation whose influence was so disquieting to the four women; still, they hoped that the Auvergnat would be too late in bringing back the person who so certainly held the first place in the widow Crochard's affections. The widow, evidently in the enjoyment of a thousand crowns a year, would not have been so fondly cherished by this feminine trio, but that neither of them, nor Francoise herself knew of her having any heir. The wealth enjoyed by Mademoiselle de Bellefeuille, whom Madame Crochard, in obedience to the traditions of the older opera, never allowed herself to speak of by the affectionate name of daughter, almost justified the four women in their scheme of dividing among themselves the old woman's "pickings."

Presently the one of these three sibyls who kept guard over the sick woman came shaking her head at the other anxious two, and said:

"It is time we should be sending for the Abbe Fontanon. In another two hours she will neither have the wit nor the strength to write a line."

Thereupon the toothless old cook went off, and returned with a man wearing a black gown. A low forehead showed a small mind in this priest, whose features were mean; his flabby, fat cheeks and double chin betrayed the easy-going egotist; his powdered hair gave him a pleasant look, till he raised his small, brown eyes, prominent under a flat forehead, and not unworthy to glitter under the brows of a Tartar.

"Monsieur l'Abbe," said Francoise, "I thank you for all your advice; but believe me, I have taken the greatest care of the dear soul."

But the servant, with her dragging step and woe-begone look, was silent when she saw that the door of the apartment was open, and that the most insinuating of the three dowagers was standing on the landing to be the first to speak with the confessor. When the priest had politely faced the honeyed and bigoted broadside of words fired off from the widow's three friends, he went into the sickroom to sit by Madame Crochard. Decency, and some sense of reserve, compelled the three women and old Francoise to remain in the sitting-room, and to make such grimaces of grief as are possible in perfection only to such wrinkled faces.

"Oh, is it not ill-luck!" cried Francoise, heaving a sigh. "This is the fourth mistress I have buried. The first left me a hundred francs a year, the second a sum of fifty crowns, and the third a thousand crowns down. After thirty years' service, that is all I have to call my own."

The woman took advantage of her freedom to come and go, to slip into a cupboard, whence she could hear the priest.

"I see with pleasure, daughter," said Fontanon, "that you have pious sentiments; you have a sacred relic round your neck."

Madame Crochard, with a feeble vagueness which seemed to show that she had not all her wits about her, pulled out the Imperial Cross of the Legion of Honor. The priest started back at seeing the Emperor's head; he went up to the penitent again, and she spoke to him, but in such a low tone that for some minutes Francoise could hear nothing.

"Woe upon me!" cried the old woman suddenly. "Do not desert me. What, Monsieur l'Abbe, do you think I shall be called to account for my daughter's soul?"

The Abbe spoke too low, and the partition was too thick for Francoise to hear the reply.

"Alas!" sobbed the woman, "the wretch has left me nothing that I can bequeath. When he robbed me of my dear Caroline, he parted us, and only allowed me three thousand francs a year, of which the capital belongs to my daughter."

"Madame has a daughter, and nothing to live on but an annuity," shrieked Francoise, bursting into the drawing-room.

The three old crones looked at each other in dismay. One of them, whose nose and chin nearly met with an expression that betrayed a superior type of hypocrisy and cunning, winked her eyes; and as soon as Francoise's back was turned, she gave her friends a nod, as much as to say, "That slut is too knowing by half; her name has figured in three wills already."

So the three old dames sat on.

However, the Abbe presently came out, and at a word from him the witches scuttered down the stairs at his heels, leaving Francoise alone with her mistress. Madame Crochard, whose sufferings increased in severity, rang, but in vain, for this woman, who only called out, "Coming, coming—in a minute!" The doors of cupboards and wardrobes were slamming as though Francoise were hunting high and low for a lost lottery ticket.

Just as this crisis was at a climax, Mademoiselle de Bellefeuille came to stand by her mother's bed, lavishing tender words on her.

"Oh my dear mother, how criminal I have been! You are ill, and I did not know it; my heart did not warn me. However, here I am—"

"Caroline—"

"What is it?"

"They fetched a priest—"

"But send for a doctor, bless me!" cried Mademoiselle de Bellefeuille. "Francoise, a doctor! How is it that these ladies never sent for a doctor?"

"They sent for a priest——" repeated the old woman with a gasp.

"She is so ill—and no soothing draught, nothing on her table!"

33

The mother made a vague sign, which Caroline's watchful eye understood, for she was silent to let her mother speak.

"They brought a priest—to hear my confession, as they said.— Beware, Caroline!" cried the old woman with an effort, "the priest made me tell him your benefactor's name."

"But who can have told you, poor mother?"

The old woman died, trying to look knowingly cunning. If Mademoiselle de Bellefeuille had noted her mother's face she might have seen what no one ever will see—Death laughing.

To enter into the interests that lay beneath this introduction to my tale, we must for a moment forget the actors in it, and look back at certain previous incidents, of which the last was closely concerned with the death of Madame Crochard. The two parts will then form a whole—a story which, by a law peculiar to life in Paris, was made up of two distinct sets of actions.

Towards the close of the month of November 1805, a young barrister, aged about six-and-twenty, was going down the stairs of the hotel where the High Chancellor of the Empire resided, at about three o'clock one morning. Having reached the courtyard in full evening dress, under a keen frost, he could not help giving vent to an exclamation of dismay—qualified, however, by the spirit which rarely deserts a Frenchman—at seeing no hackney coach waiting outside the gates, and hearing no noises such as arise from the wooden shoes or harsh voices of the hackney-coachmen of Paris. The occasional pawing of the horses of the Chief Justice's carriage— the young man having left him still playing bouillote with Cambaceres—alone rang out in the paved court, which was scarcely lighted by the carriage lamps. Suddenly the young lawyer felt a friendly hand on his shoulder, and turning round, found himself face to face with the Judge, to whom he bowed. As the footman let down the steps of his carriage, the old gentleman, who had served the Convention, suspected the junior's dilemma.

"All cats are gray in the dark," said he good-humoredly. "The

Chief Justice cannot compromise himself by putting a pleader in the right way! Especially," he went on, "when the pleader is the nephew of an old colleague, one of the lights of the grand Council of State which gave France the Napoleonic Code."

At a gesture from the chief magistrate of France under the Empire, the foot-passenger got into the carriage.

"Where do you live?" asked the great man, before the footman who awaited his orders had closed the door.

"Quai des Augustins, monseigneur."

The horses started, and the young man found himself alone with the Minister, to whom he had vainly tried to speak before and after the sumptuous dinner given by Cambaceres; in fact, the great man had evidently avoided him throughout the evening.

"Well, Monsieur de Granville, you are on the high road!"

"So long as I sit by your Excellency's side—"

"Nay, I am not jesting," said the Minister. "You were called two years since, and your defence in the case of Simeuse and Hauteserre had raised you high in your profession."

"I had supposed that my interest in those unfortunate emigres had done me no good."

"You are still very young," said the great man gravely. "But the High Chancellor," he went on, after a pause, "was greatly pleased with you this evening. Get a judgeship in the lower courts; we want men. The nephew of a man in whom Cambaceres and I take great interest must not remain in the background for lack of encouragement. Your uncle helped us to tide over a very stormy season, and services of that kind are not forgotten." The Minister sat silent for a few minutes. "Before long," he went on, "I shall have three vacancies open in the Lower Courts and in the Imperial Court in Paris. Come to see me, and take the place you prefer. Till then work hard, but do not be seen at my receptions. In the first place, I am overwhelmed with work; and besides that, your rivals may suspect your purpose and do you harm with the patron. Cambaceres and I, by not speaking a word to you this evening, have averted the accusation of favoritism."

As the great man ceased speaking, the carriage drew up on the Quai des Augustins; the young lawyer thanked his generous patron for the two lifts he had conferred on him, and then knocked at his door pretty loudly, for the bitter wind blew cold about his calves. At last the old lodgekeeper pulled up the latch; and as the young man passed his window, called out in a hoarse voice, "Monsieur Granville, here is a letter for you."

The young man took the letter, and in spite of the cold, tried to identify the writing by the gleam of a dull lamp fast dying out. "From my father!" he exclaimed, as he took his bedroom candle, which the porter at last had lighted. And he ran up to his room to read the following epistle:—

"Set off by the next mail; and if you can get here soon enough, your fortune is made. Mademoiselle Angelique Bontems has lost her sister; she is now an only child; and, as we know, she does not hate you. Madame Bontems can now leave her about forty thousand francs a year, besides whatever she may give her when she marries. I have prepared the way.

"Our friends will wonder to see a family of old nobility allying itself to the Bontems; old Bontems was a red republican of the deepest dye, owning large quantities of the nationalized land, that he bought for a mere song. But he held nothing but convent lands, and the monks will not come back; and then, as you have already so far derogated as to become a lawyer, I cannot see why we should shrink from a further concession to the prevalent ideas. The girl will have three hundred thousand francs; I can give you a hundred thousand; your mother's property must be worth fifty thousand crowns, more or less; so if you choose to take a judgeship, my dear son, you are quite in a position to become a senator as much as any other man. My brother-in-law the Councillor of State will not indeed lend you a helping-hand; still, as he is not married, his property will some day be yours, and if you are not senator by your own efforts, you will get it

through him. Then you will be perched high enough to look on at events. Farewell.

> *Yours affectionately."*

So young Granville went to bed full of schemes, each fairer than the last. Under the powerful protection of the High Chancellor, the Chief Justice, and his mother's brother—one of the originators of the Code—he was about to make a start in a coveted position before the highest court of the Empire, and he already saw himself a member of the bench whence Napoleon selected the chief functionaries of the realm. He could also promise himself a fortune handsome enough to keep up his rank, for which the slender income of five thousand francs from an estate left him by his mother would be quite insufficient.

To crown his ambitious dreams with a vision of happiness, he called up the guileless face of Mademoiselle Angelique Bontems, the companion of his childhood. Until he came to boyhood his father and mother had made no objection to his intimacy with their neighbor's pretty little daughter; but when, during his brief holiday visits to Bayeux, his parents, who prided themselves on their good birth, saw what friends the young people were, they forbade his ever thinking of her. Thus for ten years past Granville had only had occasional glimpses of the girl, whom he still sometimes thought of as "his little wife." And in those brief moments when they met free from the active watchfulness of their families, they had scarcely exchanged a few vague civilities at the church door or in the street. Their happiest days had been those when, brought together by one of those country festivities known in Normandy as Assemblees, they could steal a glance at each other from afar.

In the course of the last vacation Granville had twice seen Angelique, and her downcast eyes and drooping attitude had led him to suppose that she was crushed by some unknown tyranny.

He was off by seven next morning to the coach office in the Rue

Notre-Dame-des-Victoires, and was so lucky as to find a vacant seat in the diligence then starting for Caen.

It was not without deep emotion that the young lawyer saw once more the spires of the cathedral at Bayeux. As yet no hope of his life had been cheated, and his heart swelled with the generous feelings that expand in the youthful soul.

After the too lengthy feast of welcome prepared by his father, who awaited him with some friends, the impatient youth was conducted to a house, long familiar to him, standing in the Rue Teinture. His heart beat high when his father—still known in the town of Bayeux as the Comte de Granville—knocked loudly at a carriage gate off which the green paint was dropping in scales. It was about four in the afternoon. A young maid-servant, in a cotton cap, dropped a short curtsey to the two gentlemen, and said that the ladies would soon be home from vespers.

The Count and his son were shown into a low room used as a drawing-room, but more like a convent parlor. Polished panels of dark walnut made it gloomy enough, and around it some old-fashioned chairs covered with worsted work and stiff armchairs were symmetrically arranged. The stone chimney-shelf had no ornament but a discolored mirror, and on each side of it were the twisted branches of a pair of candle-brackets, such as were made at the time of the Peace of Utrecht. Against a panel opposite, young Granville saw an enormous crucifix of ebony and ivory surrounded by a wreath of box that had been blessed. Though there were three windows to the room, looking out on a country-town garden, laid out in formal square beds edged with box, the room was so dark that it was difficult to discern, on the wall opposite the windows, three pictures of sacred subjects painted by a skilled hand, and purchased, no doubt, during the Revolution by old Bontems, who, as governor of the district, had never neglected his opportunities. From the carefully polished floor to the green checked holland curtains everything shone with conventual cleanliness.

The young man's heart felt an involuntary chill in this silent retreat where Angelique dwelt. The habit of frequenting the glittering Paris drawing-rooms, and the constant whirl of society, had effaced from his memory the dull and peaceful surroundings of a country life, and the contrast was so startling as to give him a sort of internal shiver. To have just left a party at the house of Cambaceres, where life was so large, where minds could expand, where the splendor of the Imperial Court was so vividly reflected, and to be dropped suddenly into a sphere of squalidly narrow ideas—was it not like a leap from Italy into Greenland?—"Living here is not life!" said he to himself, as he looked round the Methodistical room. The old Count, seeing his son's dismay, went up to him, and taking his hand, led him to a window, where there was still a gleam of daylight, and while the maid was lighting the yellow tapers in the candle branches he tried to clear away the clouds that the dreary place had brought to his brow.

"Listen, my boy," said he. "Old Bontems' widow is a frenzied bigot. 'When the devil is old—' you know! I see that the place goes against the grain. Well, this is the whole truth; the old woman is priest-ridden; they have persuaded her that it was high time to make sure of heaven, and the better to secure Saint Peter and his keys she pays before-hand. She goes to Mass every day, attends every service, takes the communion every Sunday God has made, and amuses herself by restoring chapels. She had given so many ornaments, and albs, and chasubles, she has crowned the canopy with so many feathers, that on the occasion of the last Corpus Christi procession as great a crowd came together as to see a man hanged, just to stare at the priests in their splendid dresses and all the vessels regilt. This house too is a sort of Holy Land. It was I who hindered her from giving those three pictures to the Church—a Domenichino, a Correggio, and an Andrea del Sarto—worth a good deal of money."

"But Angelique?" asked the young man.

"If you do not marry her, Angelique is done for," said the Count. "Our holy apostles counsel her to live a virgin martyr. I have had the utmost difficulty in stirring up her little heart, since

39

she has been the only child, by talking to her of you; but, as you will easily understand, as soon as she is married you will carry her off to Paris. There, festivities, married life, the theatres, and the rush of Parisian society, will soon make her forget confessionals, and fasting, and hair shirts, and Masses, which are the exclusive nourishment of such creatures."

"But the fifty thousand francs a year derived from Church property? Will not all that return—"

"That is the point!" exclaimed the Count, with a cunning glance. "In consideration of this marriage—for Madame Bontems' vanity is not a little flattered by the notion of grafting the Bontems on to the genealogical tree of the Granvilles—the aforenamed mother agrees to settle her fortune absolutely on the girl, reserving only a life-interest. The priesthood, therefore, are set against the marriage; but I have had the banns published, everything is ready, and in a week you will be out of the clutches of the mother and her Abbes. You will have the prettiest girl in Bayeux, a good little soul who will give you no trouble, because she has sound principles. She has been mortified, as they say in their jargon, by fasting and prayer—and," he added in a low voice, "by her mother."

A modest tap at the door silenced the Count, who expected to see the two ladies appear. A little page came in, evidently in a great hurry; but, abashed by the presence of the two gentlemen, he beckoned to a housekeeper, who followed him. Dressed in a blue cloth jacket with short tails, and blue-and-white striped trousers, his hair cut short all round, the boy's expression was that of a chorister, so strongly was it stamped with the compulsory propriety that marks every member of a bigoted household.

"Mademoiselle Gatienne," said he, "do you know where the books are for the offices of the Virgin? The ladies of the Congregation of the Sacred Heart are going in procession this evening round the church."

Gatienne went in search of the books.

"Will they go on much longer, my little man?" asked the Count.

"Oh, half an hour at most."

"Let us go to look on," said the father to his son. "There will be some pretty women there, and a visit to the Cathedral can do us no harm."

The young lawyer followed him with a doubtful expression.

"What is the matter?" asked the Count.

"The matter, father, is that I am sure I am right."

"But you have said nothing."

"No; but I have been thinking that you have still ten thousand francs a year left of your original fortune. You will leave them to me—as long a time hence as possible, I hope. But if you are ready to give me a hundred thousand francs to make a foolish match, you will surely allow me to ask you for only fifty thousand to save me from such a misfortune, and enjoy as a bachelor a fortune equal to what your Mademoiselle Bontems would bring me."

"Are you crazy?"

"No, father. These are the facts. The Chief Justice promised me yesterday that I should have a seat on the Bench. Fifty thousand francs added to what I have, and to the pay of my appointment, will give me an income of twelve thousand francs a year. And I then shall most certainly have a chance of marrying a fortune, better than this alliance, which will be poor in happiness if rich in goods."

"It is very clear," said his father, "that you were not brought up under the old regime. Does a man of our rank ever allow his wife to be in his way?"

"But, my dear father, in these days marriage is—"

"Bless me!" cried the Count, interrupting his son, "then what my old emigre friends tell me is true, I suppose. The Revolution has left us habits devoid of pleasure, and has infected all the young men with vulgar principles. You, like my Jacobin brother-in-law, will harangue me, I suppose, on the Nation, Public Morals, and Disinterestedness!—Good Heavens! But for the Emperor's sisters, where should we be?"

The still hale old man, whom the peasants on the estate persisted in calling the Signeur de Granville, ended his speech as they entered the Cathedral porch. In spite of the sanctity of the place, and even as he dipped his fingers in the holy water, he hummed an air from the opera of Rose et Colas, and then led the way down the side aisles, stopping by each pillar to survey the rows of heads, all in lines like ranks of soldiers on parade.

The special service of the Sacred Heart was about to begin. The ladies affiliated to that congregation were in front near the choir, so the Count and his son made their way to that part of the nave, and stood leaning against one of the columns where there was least light, whence they could command a view of this mass of faces, looking like a meadow full of flowers. Suddenly, close to young Granville, a voice, sweeter than it seemed possible to ascribe to a human being, broke into song, like the first nightingale when winter is past. Though it mingled with the voices of a thousand other women and the notes of the organ, that voice stirred his nerves as though they vibrated to the too full and too piercing sounds of a harmonium. The Parisian turned round, and, seeing a young figure, though, the head being bent, her face was entirely concealed by a large white bonnet, concluded that the voice was hers. He fancied that he recognized Angelique in spite of a brown merino pelisse that wrapped her, and he nudged his father's elbow.

"Yes, there she is," said the Count, after looking where his son pointed, and then, by an expressive glance, he directed his attention to the pale face of an elderly woman who had already detected the strangers, though her false eyes, deep set in dark circles, did not seem to have strayed from the prayer-book she held.

Angelique raised her face, gazing at the altar as if to inhale the heavy scent of the incense that came wafted in clouds over the two women. And then, in the doubtful light that the tapers shed down the nave, with that of a central lamp and of some lights round the pillars, the young man beheld a face which shook his determination. A white watered-silk bonnet closely framed features of perfect regularity, the oval being completed by the satin ribbon tie that fastened it under her dimpled chin. Over her forehead, very sweet though low, hair of a pale gold color parted in two bands and fell over her cheeks, like the shadow of leaves on a flower. The arches of her eyebrows were drawn with the accuracy we admire in the best Chinese paintings. Her nose, almost aquiline in profile, was exceptionally firmly cut, and her lips were like two rose lines lovingly traced with a delicate brush. Her eyes, of a light blue, were expressive of innocence.

Though Granville discerned a sort of rigid reserve in this girlish face, he could ascribe it to the devotion in which Angelique was rapt. The solemn words of prayer, visible in the cold, came from between rows of pearls, like a fragrant mist, as it were. The young man involuntarily bent over her a little to breathe this diviner air. This movement attracted the girl's notice; her gaze, raised to the altar, was diverted to Granville, whom she could see but dimly in the gloom; but she recognized him as the companion of her youth, and a memory more vivid than prayer brought a supernatural glow to her face; she blushed. The young lawyer was thrilled with joy at seeing the hopes of another life overpowered by those of love, and the glory of the sanctuary eclipsed by earthly reminiscences; but his triumph was brief. Angelique dropped her veil, assumed a calm demeanor, and went on singing without letting her voice betray the least emotion.

Granville was a prey to one single wish, and every thought of prudence vanished. By the time the service was ended, his impatience was so great that he could not leave the ladies to go home alone, but came at once to make his bow to "his little wife." They bashfully greeted each other in the Cathedral porch in the presence of the congregation. Madame Bontems was tremulous with pride as she took the Comte de Granville's arm, though he, forced to offer it in the presence of all the world was vexed enough with his son for his ill-advised impatience.

For about a fortnight, between the official announcement of the intended marriage of the Vicomte de Granville to Mademoiselle Bontems and the solemn day of the wedding, he came assiduously to visit his lady-love in the dismal drawing-room, to which he became accustomed. His long calls were devoted to watching Angelique's character; for his prudence, happily, had made itself heard again in the day after their first meeting. He always found her seated at a little table of some West Indian wood, and engaged in marking the linen of her trousseau. Angelique never spoke first on the subject of religion. If the young lawyer amused himself with fingering the handsome rosary that she kept in a little green velvet bag, if he laughed as he looked at a relic such as usually is attached to this means of grace, Angelique would gently take the rosary out of his hands and replace it in the bag without a word, putting it away at once. When, now and then, Granville was so bold as to make mischievous remarks as to certain religious practices, the pretty girl listened to him with the obstinate smile of assurance.

"You must either believe nothing, or believe everything the Church teaches," she would say. "Would you wish to have a woman without a religion as the mother of your children?—No.— What man may dare judge as between disbelievers and God? And how can I then blame what the Church allows?"

Angelique appeared to be animated by such fervent charity, the young man saw her look at him with such perfect conviction, that he sometimes felt tempted to embrace her religious views; her firm belief that she was in the only right road aroused doubts in his mind, which she tried to turn to account.

But then Granville committed the fatal blunder of mistaking the enchantment of desire for that of love. Angelique was so happy in reconciling the voice of her heart with that of duty, by giving way to a liking that had grown up with her from childhood, that the deluded man could not discern which of the two spoke the louder. Are not all young men ready to trust the promise of a pretty face and to infer beauty of soul from beauty of feature? An indefinable impulse leads them to believe that moral perfection must co-exist with physical perfection. If Angelique had not been at liberty to give vent to her sentiments, they would soon have dried up in her heart like a plant watered with some deadly acid. How should a lover be aware of bigotry so well hidden?

This was the course of young Granville's feelings during that fortnight, devoured by him like a book of which the end is absorbing. Angelique, carefully watched by him, seemed the gentlest of creatures, and he even caught himself feeling grateful to Madame Bontems, who, by implanting so deeply the principles of religion, had in some degree inured her to meet the troubles of life.

On the day named for signing the inevitable contract, Madame Bontems made her son-in-law pledge himself solemnly to respect her daughter's religious practices, to allow her entire liberty of conscience, to permit her to go to communion, to church, to confession as often as she pleased, and never to control her choice of priestly advisers. At this critical moment Angelique looked at her future husband with such pure and innocent eyes, that Granville did not hesitate to give his word. A smile puckered the lips of the Abbe Fontanon, a pale man, who directed the consciences of this household. Mademoiselle Bontems, by a slight nod, seemed to promise that she would never take an unfair advantage of this freedom. As to the old Count, he gently whistled the tune of an old song, Va-t-en-voir s'ils viennent ("Go and see if they are coming on!")

A few days after the wedding festivities of which so much is thought in the provinces, Granville and his wife went to Paris, whither the young man was recalled by his appointment as public prosecutor to the Supreme Court of the Seine circuit.

When the young couple set out to find a residence, Angelique used the influence that the honeymoon gives to every wife in persuading her husband to take a large apartment in the ground-floor of a house at the corner of the Vieille Rue du Temple and the Rue Nueve Saint-Francois. Her chief reason for this choice was that the house was close to the Rue d'Orleans, where there was a church, and not far from a small chapel in the Rue Saint-Louis.

"A good housewife provides for everything," said her husband, laughing.

Angelique pointed out to him that this part of Paris, known as the Marais, was within easy reach of the Palais de Justice, and that the lawyers they knew lived in the neighborhood. A fairly large garden made the apartment particularly advantageous to a young couple; the children—if Heaven should send them any—could play in the open air; the courtyard was spacious, and there were good stables.

The lawyer wished to live in the Chaussee d'Antin, where everything is fresh and bright, where the fashions may be seen while still new, where a well-dressed crowd throngs the Boulevards, and the distance is less to the theatres or places of amusement; but he was obliged to give way to the coaxing ways of a young wife, who asked this as his first favor; so, to please her, he settled in the Marais. Granville's duties required him to work hard—all the more, because they were new to him—so he devoted himself in the first place to furnishing his private study and arranging his books. He was soon established in a room crammed with papers, and left the decoration of the house to his wife. He was all the better pleased to plunge Angelique into the bustle of buying furniture and fittings, the source of so much pleasure and of so many associations to most young women, because he was rather ashamed of depriving her of his company more often than the usages of early married life require. As soon as his work was fairly under way, he gladly allowed his wife to tempt him out of his study to consider the effect of furniture or hangings, which he had before only seen piecemeal or unfinished.

If the old adage is true that says a woman may be judged of from her front door, her rooms must express her mind with even greater fidelity. Madame de Granville had perhaps stamped the various things she had ordered with the seal of her own character; the young lawyer was certainly startled by the cold, arid solemnity that reigned in these rooms; he found nothing to charm his taste; everything was discordant, nothing gratified the eye. The rigid mannerism that prevailed in the sitting-room at Bayeux had invaded his home; the broad panels were hollowed in circles, and decorated with those arabesques of which the long, monotonous mouldings are in such bad taste. Anxious to find excuses for his wife, the young husband began again, looking first at the long and lofty ante-room through which the apartment was entered. The color of the panels, as ordered by his wife, was too heavy, and the very dark green velvet used to cover the benches added to the gloom of this entrance—not, to be sure, an important room, but giving a first impression—just as we measure a man's intelligence by his first address. An ante-room is a kind of preface which announces what is to follow, but promises nothing.

The young husband wondered whether his wife could really have chosen the lamp of an antique pattern, which hung in the centre of this bare hall, the pavement of black and white marble, and the paper in imitation of blocks of stone, with green moss on them in places. A handsome, but not new, barometer hung on the middle of one of the walls, as if to accentuate the void. At the sight of it all, he looked round at his wife; he saw her so much pleased by the red braid binding to the cotton curtains, so satisfied with the barometer and the strictly decent statue that ornamented a large Gothic stove, that he had not the barbarous courage to overthrow such deep convictions. Instead of blaming his wife, Granville blamed himself, accusing himself of having failed in his duty of guiding the first steps in Paris of a girl brought up at Bayeux.

From this specimen, what might not be expected of the other rooms? What was to be looked for from a woman who took fright at the bare legs of a Caryatid, and who would not look at a chandelier or a candle-stick if she saw on it the nude outlines of an Egyptian bust? At this date the school of David was at the height of its glory; all the art of France bore the stamp of his correct design and his love of antique types, which indeed gave his pictures the character of colored sculpture. But none of these devices of Imperial luxury found civic rights under Madame de Granville's roof. The spacious, square drawing-room remained as it had been left from the time of Louis XV., in white and tarnished gold, lavishly adorned by the architect with checkered lattice-work and the hideous garlands due to the uninventive designers of the time. Still, if harmony at least had prevailed, if the furniture of modern mahogany had but assumed the twisted forms of which Boucher's corrupt taste first set the fashion, Angelique's room would only have suggested the fantastic contrast of a young couple in the nineteenth century living as though they were in the eighteenth; but a number of details were in ridiculous discord. The consoles, the clocks, the candelabra, were decorated with the military trophies which the wars of the Empire commended to the affections of the Parisians; and the Greek helmets, the Roman crossed daggers, and the shields so dear to military enthusiasm that they were introduced on furniture of the most peaceful uses, had no fitness side by side with the delicate and profuse arabesques that delighted Madame de Pompadour.

Bigotry tends to an indescribably tiresome kind of humility which does not exclude pride. Whether from modesty or by choice, Madame de Granville seemed to have a horror of light and cheerful colors; perhaps, too, she imagined that brown and purple beseemed the dignity of a magistrate. How could a girl accustomed to an austere life have admitted the luxurious divans that may suggest evil thoughts, the elegant and tempting boudoirs where naughtiness may be imagined?

The poor husband was in despair. From the tone in which he approved, only seconding the praises she bestowed on herself, Angelique understood that nothing really pleased him; and she expressed so much regret at her want of success, that Granville, who was very much in love, regarded her disappointment as a proof of her affection instead of resentment for an offence to her self-conceit. After all, could he expect a girl just snatched from the humdrum of country notions, with no experience of the niceties and grace of Paris life, to know or do any better? Rather would he believe that his wife's choice had been overruled by the tradesmen than allow himself to own the truth. If he had been less in love, he would have understood that the dealers, always quick to discern their customers' ideas, had blessed Heaven for sending them a tasteless little bigot, who would take their old-fashioned goods off their hands. So he comforted the pretty provincial.

"Happiness, dear Angelique, does not depend on a more or less elegant piece of furniture; it depends on the wife's sweetness, gentleness, and love."

"Why, it is my duty to love you," said Angelique mildly, "and I can have no more delightful duty to carry out."

Nature has implanted in the heart of woman so great a desire to please, so deep a craving for love, that, even in a youthful bigot, the ideas of salvation and a future existence must give way to the happiness of early married life. And, in fact, from the month of April, when they were married, till the beginning of winter, the husband and wife lived in perfect union. Love and hard work have the grace of making a man tolerably indifferent to external matters. Being obliged to spend half the day in court fighting for the gravest interests of men's lives or fortunes, Granville was less alive than another might have been to certain facts in his household.

If, on a Friday, he found none but Lenten fare, and by chance asked for a dish of meat without getting it, his wife, forbidden by the Gospel to tell a lie, could still, by such subterfuges as are permissible in the interests of religion, cloak what was premeditated purpose under some pretext of her own carelessness or the scarcity in the market. She would often exculpate herself at the expense of the cook, and even go so far as to scold him. At that time young lawyers did not, as they do now, keep the fasts of the Church, the four rogation seasons, and the vigils of festivals; so

Granville was not at first aware of the regular recurrence of these Lenten meals, which his wife took care should be made dainty by the addition of teal, moor-hen, and fish-pies, that their amphibious meat or high seasoning might cheat his palate. Thus the young man unconsciously lived in strict orthodoxy, and worked out his salvation without knowing it.

On week-days he did not know whether his wife went to Mass or no. On Sundays, with very natural amiability, he accompanied her to church to make up to her, as it were, for sometimes giving up vespers in favor of his company; he could not at first fully enter into the strictness of his wife's religious views. The theatres being impossible in summer by reason of the heat, Granville had not even the opportunity of the great success of a piece to give rise to the serious question of play-going. And, in short, at the early stage of a union to which a man has been led by a young girl's beauty, he can hardly be exacting as to his amusements. Youth is greedy rather than dainty, and possession has a charm in itself. How should he be keen to note coldness, dignity, and reserve in the woman to whom he ascribes the excitement he himself feels, and lends the glow of the fire that burns within him? He must have attained a certain conjugal calm before he discovers that a bigot sits waiting for love with her arms folded.

Granville, therefore, believed himself happy till a fatal event brought its influence to bear on his married life. In the month of November 1808 the Canon of Bayeux Cathedral who had been the keeper of Madame Bontems' conscience and her daughter's, came to Paris, spurred by the ambition to be at the head of a church in the capital—a position which he regarded perhaps as the stepping-stone to a bishopric. On resuming his former control of this wandering lamb, he was horrified to find her already so much deteriorated by the air of Paris, and strove to reclaim her to his chilly fold. Frightened by the exhortations of this priest, a man of about eight-and-thirty, who brought with him, into the circle of the enlightened and tolerant Paris clergy, the bitter provincial catholicism and the inflexible bigotry which fetter timid souls with endless exactions, Madame de Granville did penance and returned from her Jansenist errors.

It would be tiresome to describe minutely all the circumstances which insensibly brought disaster on this household; it will be enough to relate the simple facts without giving them in strict order of time.

The first misunderstanding between the young couple was, however, a serious one.

When Granville took his wife into society she never declined solemn functions, such as dinners, concerts, or parties given by the Judges superior to her husband in the legal profession; but for a long time she constantly excused herself on the plea of a sick headache when they were invited to a ball. One day Granville, out of patience with these assumed indispositions, destroyed a note of invitation to a ball at the house of a Councillor of State, and gave his wife only a verbal invitation. Then, on the evening, her health being quite above suspicion, he took her to a magnificent entertainment.

"My dear," said he, on their return home, seeing her wear an offensive air of depression, "your position as a wife, the rank you hold in society, and the fortune you enjoy, impose on you certain duties of which no divine law can relieve you. Are you not your husband's pride? You are required to go to balls when I go, and to appear in a becoming manner."

"And what is there, my dear, so disastrous in my dress?"

"It is your manner, my dear. When a young man comes up to speak to you, you look so serious that a spiteful person might believe you doubtful of your own virtue. You seem to fear lest a smile should undo you. You really look as if you were asking forgiveness of God for the sins that may be committed around you. The world, my dearest, is not a convent.—But, as you mentioned your dress, I may confess to you that it is no less a duty to conform to the customs and fashions of Society."

"Do you wish that I should display my shape like those indecent women who wear gowns so low that impudent eyes can stare at their bare shoulders and their—"

"There is a difference, my dear," said her husband, interrupting her, "between uncovering your whole bust and giving some grace to your dress. You wear three rows of net frills that cover your throat up to your chin. You look as if you had desired your dressmaker to destroy the graceful line of your shoulders and bosom with as much care as a coquette would devote to obtaining from hers a bodice that might emphasize her covered form. Your bust is wrapped in so many folds that every one was laughing at your affectation of prudery. You would be really grieved if I were to repeat the ill-natured remarks made on your appearance."

"Those who admire such obscenity will not have to bear the burthen if we sin," said the lady tartly.

"And you did not dance?" asked Granville.

"I shall never dance," she replied.

"If I tell you that you ought to dance!" said her husband sharply. "Yes, you ought to follow the fashions, to wear flowers in your hair, and diamonds. Remember, my dear, that rich people—and we are rich—are obliged to keep up luxury in the State. Is it not far better to encourage manufacturers than to distribute money in the form of alms through the medium of the clergy?"

"You talk as a statesman!" said Angelique.

"And you as a priest," he retorted.

The discussion was bitter. Madame de Granville's answers, though spoken very sweetly and in a voice as clear as a church bell, showed an obstinacy that betrayed priestly influence. When she appealed to the rights secured to her by Granville's promise, she added that her director specially forbade her going to balls; then her husband pointed out to her that the priest was overstepping the regulations of the Church.

This odious theological dispute was renewed with great violence and acerbity on both sides when Granville proposed to take his wife to the play. Finally, the lawyer, whose sole aim was to defeat the pernicious influence exerted over his wife by her old confessor, placed the question on such a footing that Madame de Granville, in a spirit of defiance, referred it by writing to the Court of Rome, asking in so many words whether a woman could wear low gowns and go to the play and to balls without compromising her salvation.

The reply of the venerable Pope Pius VII. came at once, strongly condemning the wife's recalcitrancy and blaming the priest. This letter, a chapter on conjugal duties, might have been dictated by the spirit of Fenelon, whose grace and tenderness pervaded every line.

"A wife is right to go wherever her husband may take her. Even if she sins by his command, she will not be ultimately held answerable." These two sentences of the Pope's homily only made Madame de Granville and her director accuse him of irreligion.

But before this letter had arrived, Granville had discovered the strict observance of fast days that his wife forced upon him, and gave his servants orders to serve him with meat every day in the year. However much annoyed his wife might be by these commands, Granville, who cared not a straw for such indulgence or abstinence, persisted with manly determination.

Is it not an offence to the weakest creature that can think at all to be compelled to do, by the will of another, anything that he would otherwise have done simply of his own accord? Of all forms of tyranny, the most odious is that which constantly robs the soul of the merit of its thoughts and deeds. It has to abdicate without having reigned. The word we are readiest to speak, the feelings we most love to express, die when we are commanded to utter them.

Ere long the young man ceased to invite his friends, to give parties or dinners; the house might have been shrouded in crape. A house where the mistress is a bigot has an atmosphere of its own. The servants, who are, of course, under her immediate control, are chosen among a class who call themselves pious, and who have an unmistakable physiognomy. Just as the jolliest fellow alive, when he joins the gendarmerie, has the countenance of a gendarme, so those who give themselves over to the habit of lowering their eyes and preserving a sanctimonious mien clothes them in a livery of hypocrisy which rogues can affect to perfection.

And besides, bigots constitute a sort of republic; they all know each other; the servants they recommend and hand on from one to another are a race apart, and preserved by them, as horse-breeders will admit no animal into their stables that has not a pedigree. The more the impious—as they are thought—come to understand a household of bigots, the more they perceive that everything is stamped with an indescribable squalor; they find there, at the same time, an appearance of avarice and mystery, as in a miser's home, and the dank scent of cold incense which gives a chill to the stale atmosphere of a chapel. This methodical meanness, this narrowness of thought, which is visible in every detail, can only be expressed by one word—Bigotry. In these sinister and pitiless houses Bigotry is written on the furniture, the prints, the pictures; speech is bigoted, the silence is bigoted, the faces are those of bigots. The transformation of men and things into bigotry is an inexplicable mystery, but the fact is evident. Everybody can see that bigots do not walk, do not sit, do not speak, as men of the world walk, sit, and speak. Under their roof every one is ill at ease, no one laughs, stiffness and formality infect everything, from the mistress' cap down to her pincushion; eyes are not honest, the folks are more like shadows, and the lady of the house seems perched on a throne of ice.

One morning poor Granville discerned with grief and pain that all the symptoms of bigotry had invaded his home. There are in the world different spheres in which the same effects are seen though produced by dissimilar causes. Dulness hedges such miserable homes round with walls of brass, enclosing the horrors of the desert and the infinite void. The home is not so much a tomb as that far worse thing—a convent. In the center of this icy sphere the lawyer could study his wife dispassionately. He observed, not without keen regret, the narrow-mindedness that stood confessed in the very way that her hair grew, low on the forehead, which was slightly depressed; he discovered in the perfect regularity of her features a certain set rigidity which before long made him hate the assumed sweetness that had bewitched him. Intuition told him that one day of disaster those thin lips might say, "My dear, it is for your good!"

Madame de Granville's complexion was acquiring a dull pallor and an austere expression that were a kill-joy to all who came near her. Was this change wrought by the ascetic habits of a pharisaism which is not piety any more than avarice is economy? It would be hard to say. Beauty without expression is perhaps an imposture. This imperturbable set smile that the young wife always wore when she looked at Granville seemed to be a sort of Jesuitical formula of happiness, by which she thought to satisfy all the requirements of married life. Her charity was an offence, her soulless beauty was monstrous to those who knew her; the mildness of her speech was an irritation: she acted, not on feeling, but on duty.

There are faults which may yield in a wife to the stern lessons of experience, or to a husband's warnings; but nothing can counteract false ideas of religion. An eternity of happiness to be won, set in the scale against worldly enjoyment, triumphs over everything and makes every pang endurable. Is it not the apotheosis of egotism, of Self beyond the grave? Thus even the Pope was censured at the tribunal of the priest and the young devotee. To be always in the right is a feeling which absorbs every other in these tyrannous souls.

For some time past a secret struggle had been going on between the ideas of the husband and wife, and the young man was soon weary of a battle to which there could be no end. What man, what temper, can endure the sight of a hypocritically affectionate face and categorical resistance to his slightest wishes? What is to be done with a wife who takes advantage of his passion to protect her coldness, who seems determined on being blandly inexorable, prepares herself ecstatically to play the martyr, and looks on her husband as a scourge from God, a means of flagellation that may spare her the fires of purgatory? What picture can give an idea of these women who make virtue hateful by defying the gentle precepts of that faith which Saint John epitomized in the words, "Love one another"?

If there was a bonnet to be found in a milliner's shop that was condemned to remain in the window, or to be packed off to the colonies, Granville was certain to see it on his wife's head; if a material of bad color or hideous design were to be found, she would select it. These hapless bigots are heart-breaking in their notions of dress. Want of taste is a defect inseparable from false pietism.

And so, in the home-life that needs the fullest sympathy, Granville had no true companionship. He went out alone to parties and the theatres. Nothing in his house appealed to him. A huge Crucifix that hung between his bed and Angelique's seemed figurative of his destiny. Does it not represent a murdered Divinity, a Man-God, done to death in all the prime of life and beauty? The ivory of that cross was less cold than Angelique crucifying her husband under the plea of virtue. This it was that lay at the root of their woes; the young wife saw nothing but duty where she should have given love. Here, one Ash Wednesday, rose the pale and spectral form of Fasting in Lent, of Total Abstinence, commanded in a severe tone—and Granville did not deem it advisable to write in his turn to the Pope and take the opinion of the Consistory on the proper way of observing Lent, the Ember days, and the eve of great festivals.

His misfortune was too great! He could not even complain, for what could he say? He had a pretty young wife attached to her duties, virtuous—nay, a model of all the virtues. She had a child every year, nursed them herself, and brought them up in the highest principles. Being charitable, Angelique was promoted to rank as an angel. The old women who constituted the circle in which she moved—for at that time it was not yet "the thing" for young women to be religious as a matter of fashion—all admired Madame de Granville's piety, and regarded her, not indeed as a virgin, but as a martyr. They blamed not the wife's scruples, but the barbarous philoprogenitiveness of the husband.

Granville, by insensible degrees, overdone with work, bereft of conjugal consolations, and weary of a world in which he wandered alone, by the time he was two-and-thirty had sunk into the Slough of Despond. He hated life. Having too lofty a notion of the responsibilities imposed on him by his position to set the example of a dissipated life, he tried to deaden feeling by hard study, and began a great book on Law.

But he was not allowed to enjoy the monastic peace he had hoped for. When the celestial Angelique saw him desert worldly society to work at home with such regularity, she tried to convert him. It had been a real sorrow to her to know that her husband's opinions were not strictly Christian; and she sometimes wept as she reflected that if her husband should die it would be in a state of final impenitence, so that she could not hope to snatch him from the eternal fires of Hell. Thus Granville was a mark for the mean ideas, the vacuous arguments, the narrow views by which his wife—fancying she had achieved the first victory—tried to gain a second by bringing him back within the pale of the Church.

This was the last straw. What can be more intolerable than the blind struggle in which the obstinacy of a bigot tries to meet the acumen of a lawyer? What more terrible to endure than the acrimonious pin-pricks to which a passionate soul prefers a dagger-thrust? Granville neglected his home. Everything there was unendurable. His children, broken by their mother's frigid despotism, dared not go with him to the play; indeed, Granville could never give them any pleasure without bringing down punishment from their terrible mother. His loving nature was weaned to indifference, to a selfishness worse than death. His boys, indeed, he saved from this hell by sending them to school at an early age, and insisting on his right to train them. He rarely interfered between his wife and her daughters; but he was resolved that they should marry as soon as they were old enough.

Even if he had wished to take violent measures, he could have found no justification; his wife, backed by a formidable army of dowagers, would have had him condemned by the whole world. Thus Granville had no choice but to live in complete isolation; but, crushed under the tyranny of misery, he could not himself bear to see how altered he was by grief and toil. And he dreaded any connection or intimacy with women of the world, having no hope of finding any consolation.

The improving history of this melancholy household gave rise to no events worthy of record during the fifteen years between 1806 and 1825. Madame de Granville was exactly the same after losing her husband's affection as she had been during the time when she called herself happy. She paid for Masses, beseeching God and the Saints to enlighten her as to what the faults were which displeased her husband, and to show her the way to restore the erring sheep; but the more fervent her prayers, the less was Granville to be seen at home.

For about five years now, having achieved a high position as a judge, Granville had occupied the entresol of the house to avoid living with the Comtesse de Granville. Every morning a little scene took place, which, if evil tongues are to be believed, is repeated in many households as the result of incompatibility of temper, of moral or physical malady, or of antagonisms leading to such disaster as is recorded in this history. At about eight in the morning a housekeeper, bearing no small resemblance to a nun, rang at the Comte de Granville's door. Admitted to the room next to the

Judge's study, she always repeated the same message to the footman, and always in the same tone:

"Madame would be glad to know whether Monsieur le Comte has had a good night, and if she is to have the pleasure of his company at breakfast."

"Monsieur presents his compliments to Madame la Comtesse," the valet would say, after speaking with his master, "and begs her to hold him excused; important business compels him to be in court this morning."

A minute later the woman reappeared and asked on madame's behalf whether she would have the pleasure of seeing Monsieur le Comte before he went out.

"He is gone," was always the rely, though often his carriage was still waiting.

This little dialogue by proxy became a daily ceremonial. Granville's servant, a favorite with his master, and the cause of more than one quarrel over his irreligious and dissipated conduct, would even go into his master's room, as a matter of form, when the Count was not there, and come back with the same formula in reply.

The aggrieved wife was always on the watch for her husband's return, and standing on the steps so as to meet him like an embodiment of remorse. The petty aggressiveness which lies at the root of the monastic temper was the foundation of Madame de Granville's; she was now five-and-thirty, and looked forty. When the count was compelled by decency to speak to his wife or to dine at home, she was only too well pleased to inflict her company upon him, with her acid-sweet remarks and the intolerable dulness of her narrow-minded circle, and she tried to put him in the wrong before the servants and her charitable friends.

When, at this time, the post of President in a provincial court was offered to the Comte de Granville, who was in high favor, he begged to be allowed to remain in Paris. This refusal, of which the Keeper of the Seals alone knew the reasons, gave rise to extraordinary conjectures on the part of the Countess' intimate friends and of her director. Granville, a rich man with a hundred thousand francs a year, belonged to one of the first families of Normandy. His appointment to be Presiding Judge would have been the stepping-stone to a peer's seat; whence this strange lack of ambition? Why had he given up his great book on Law? What was the meaning of the dissipation which for nearly six years had made him a stranger to his home, his family, his study, to all he ought to hold dear? The Countess' confessor, who based his hopes of a bishopric quite as much on the families he governed as on the services he rendered to an association of which he was an ardent propagator, was much disappointed by Granville's refusal, and tried to insinuate calumnious explanations: "If Monsieur le Comte had such an objection to provincial life, it was perhaps because he dreaded finding himself under the necessity of leading a regular life, compelled to set an example of moral conduct, and to live with the Countess, from whom nothing could have alienated him but some illicit connection; for how could a woman so pure as Madame de Granville ever tolerate the disorderly life into which her husband had drifted?" The sanctimonious woman accepted as facts these hints, which unluckily were not merely hypothetical, and Madame de Granville was stricken as by a thunderbolt.

Angelique, knowing nothing of the world, of love and its follies, was so far from conceiving of any conditions of married life unlike those that had alienated her husband as possible, that she believed him to be incapable of the errors which are crimes in the eyes of any wife. When the Count ceased to demand anything of her, she imagined that the tranquillity he now seemed to enjoy was in the course of nature; and, as she had really given to him all the love which her heart was capable of feeling for a man, while the priest's conjectures were the utter destruction of the illusions she had hitherto cherished, she defended her husband; at the same time, she could not eradicate the suspicion that had been so ingeniously sown in her soul.

These alarms wrought such havoc in her feeble brain that they made her ill; she was worn by low fever. These incidents took place during Lent 1822; she would not pretermit her austerities, and fell into a decline that put her life in danger. Granville's indifference was added torture; his care and attention were such as a nephew feels himself bound to give to some old uncle.

Though the Countess had given up her persistent nagging and remonstrances, and tried to receive her husband with affectionate words, the sharpness of the bigot showed through, and one speech would often undo the work of a week.

Towards the end of May, the warm breath of spring, and more nourishing diet than her Lenten fare, restored Madame de Granville to a little strength. One morning, on coming home from Mass, she sat down on a stone bench in the little garden, where the sun's kisses reminded her of the early days of her married life, and she looked back across the years to see wherein she might have failed in her duty as a wife and mother. She was broken in upon by the Abbe Fontanon in an almost indescribable state of excitement.

"Has any misfortune befallen you, Father?" she asked with filial solicitude.

"Ah! I only wish," cried the Normandy priest, "that all the woes inflicted on you by the hand of God were dealt out to me; but, my admirable friend, there are trials to which you can but bow."

"Can any worse punishments await me than those with which Providence crushes me by making my husband the instrument of His wrath?"

"You must prepare yourself, daughter, to yet worse mischief than we and your pious friends had ever conceived of."

"Then I may thank God," said the Countess, "for vouchsafing to use you as the messenger of His will, and thus, as ever, setting the treasures of mercy by the side of the scourges of His wrath, just as in bygone days He showed a spring to Hagar when He had driven her into the desert."

"He measures your sufferings by the strength of your resignation and the weight of your sins."

"Speak; I am ready to hear!" As she said it she cast her eyes up to heaven. "Speak, Monsieur Fontanon."

"For seven years Monsieur Granville has lived in sin with a concubine, by whom he has two children; and on this adulterous connection he has spent more than five hundred thousand francs, which ought to have been the property of his legitimate family."

"I must see it to believe it!" cried the Countess.

"Far be it from you!" exclaimed the Abbe. "You must forgive, my daughter, and wait in patience and prayer till God enlightens your husband; unless, indeed, you choose to adopt against him the means offered you by human laws."

The long conversation that ensued between the priest and his penitent resulted in an extraordinary change in the Countess; she abruptly dismissed him, called her servants who were alarmed at her flushed face and crazy energy. She ordered her carriage—countermanded it—changed her mind twenty times in the hour; but at last, at about three o'clock, as if she had come to some great determination, she went out, leaving the whole household in amazement at such a sudden transformation.

"Is the Count coming home to dinner?" she asked of his servant, to whom she would never speak.

"No, madame."

"Did you go with him to the Courts this morning?"

"Yes, madame."

"And to-day is Monday?"

"Yes, madame."

"Then do the Courts sit on Mondays nowadays?"

"Devil take you!" cried the man, as his mistress drove off after saying to the coachman:

"Rue Taitbout."

Mademoiselle de Bellefeuille was weeping: Roger, sitting by her side, held one of her hands between his own. He was silent, looking by turns at little Charles—who, not understanding his mother's grief, stood speechless at the sight of her tears—at the cot where Eugenie lay sleeping, and Caroline's face, on which grief had the effect of rain falling across the beams of cheerful sunshine.

"Yes, my darling," said Roger, after a long silence, "that is the great secret: I am married. But some day I hope we may form but one family. My wife has been given over ever since last March. I do not wish her dead; still, if it should please God to take her to Himself, I believe she will be happier in Paradise than in a world to whose griefs and pleasures she is equally indifferent."

"How I hate that woman! How could she bear to make you unhappy? And yet it is to that unhappiness that I owe my happiness!"

Her tears suddenly ceased.

"Caroline, let us hope," cried Roger. "Do not be frightened by anything that priest may have said to you. Though my wife's confessor is a man to be feared for his power in the congregation, if he should try to blight our happiness I would find means—"

"What could you do?"

"We would go to Italy: I would fly—"

A shriek that rang out from the adjoining room made Roger start and Mademoiselle de Bellefeuille quake; but she rushed into the drawing-room, and there found Madame de Granville in a dead faint. When the Countess recovered her senses, she sighed deeply on finding herself supported by the Count and her rival, whom she instinctively pushed away with a gesture of contempt. Mademoiselle de Bellefeuille rose to withdraw.

"You are at home, madame," said Granville, taking Caroline by the arm. "Stay."

The Judge took up his wife in his arms, carried her to the carriage, and got into it with her.

"Who is it that has brought you to the point of wishing me dead, of resolving to fly?" asked the Countess, looking at her husband with grief mingled with indignation. "Was I not young? you thought me pretty—what fault have you to find with me? Have I been false to you? Have I not been a virtuous and well-conducted wife? My heart has cherished no image but yours, my ears have listened to no other voice. What duty have I failed in? What have I ever denied you?"

"Happiness, madame," said the Count severely. "You know, madame, that there are two ways of serving God. Some Christians imagine that by going to church at fixed hours to say a Paternoster, by attending Mass regularly and avoiding sin, they may win heaven—but they, madame, will go to hell; they have not loved God for himself, they have not worshiped Him as He chooses to be worshiped, they have made no sacrifice. Though mild in seeming, they are hard on their neighbors; they see the law, the letter, not the spirit.—This is how you have treated me, your earthly husband; you have sacrificed my happiness to your salvation; you were always absorbed in prayer when I came to you in gladness of heart; you wept when you should have cheered my toil; you have never tried to satisfy any demands I have made on you."

"And if they were wicked," cried the Countess hotly, "was I to lose my soul to please you?"

"It is a sacrifice which another, a more loving woman, has dared to make," said Granville coldly.

"Dear God!" she cried, bursting into tears, "Thou hearest! Has he been worthy of the prayers and penance I have lived in, wearing myself out to atone for his sins and my own?—Of what avail is virtue?"

"To win Heaven, my dear. A woman cannot be at the same time the wife of a man and the spouse of Christ. That would be bigamy; she must choose between a husband and a nunnery. For the sake of future advantage you have stripped your soul of all the love, all the devotion, which God commands that you should have for me, you have cherished no feeling but hatred—"

"Have I not loved you?" she put in.

"No, madame."

"Then what is love?" the Countess involuntarily inquired.

"Love, my dear," replied Granville, with a sort of ironical surprise, "you are incapable of understanding it. The cold sky of Normandy is not that of Spain. This difference of climate is no doubt the secret of our disaster.—To yield to our caprices, to guess them, to find pleasure in pain, to sacrifice the world's opinion, your pride, your religion even, and still regard these offerings as mere grains of incense burnt in honor of the idol—that is love—"

"The love of ballet-girls!" cried the Countess in horror. "Such flames cannot last, and must soon leave nothing but ashes and cinders, regret or despair. A wife ought, in my opinion, to bring you true friendship, equable warmth—"

"You speak of warmth as negroes speak of ice," retorted the Count, with a sardonic smile. "Consider that the humblest daisy has more charms than the proudest and most gorgeous of the red hawthorns that attract us in spring by their strong scent and brilliant color.—At the same time," he went on, "I will do you justice. You have kept so precisely in the straight path of imaginary duty prescribed by law, that only to make you understand wherein you have failed towards me, I should be obliged to enter into details which would offend your dignity, and instruct you in matters which would seem to you to undermine all morality."

"And you dare to speak of morality when you have but just left the house where you have dissipated your children's fortune in debaucheries?" cried the Countess, maddened by her husband's reticence.

"There, madame, I must correct you," said the Count, coolly interrupting his wife. "Though Mademoiselle de Bellefeuille is rich, it is at nobody's expense. My uncle was master of his fortune, and had several heirs. In his lifetime, and out of pure friendship, regarding her as his niece, he gave her the little estate of Bellefeuille. As for anything else, I owe it to his liberality—"

"Such conduct is only worthy of a Jacobin!" said the sanctimonious Angelique.

"Madame, you are forgetting that your own father was one of the Jacobins whom you scorn so uncharitably," said the Count severely. "Citizen Bontems was signing death-warrants at a time when my uncle was doing France good service."

Madame de Granville was silenced. But after a short pause, the remembrance of what she had just seen reawakened in her soul the jealousy which nothing can kill in a woman's heart, and she murmured, as if to herself—"How can a woman thus destroy her own soul and that of others?"

"Bless me, madame," replied the Count, tired of this dialogue, "you yourself may some day have to answer that question." The Countess was scared. "You perhaps will be held excused by the merciful Judge, who will weigh our sins," he went on, "in consideration of the conviction with which you have worked out my misery. I do not hate you—I hate those who have perverted your heart and your reason. You have prayed for me, just as

Mademoiselle de Bellefeuille has given me her heart and crowned my life with love. You should have been my mistress and the prayerful saint by turns.—Do me the justice to confess that I am no reprobate, no debauchee. My life was cleanly. Alas! after seven years of wretchedness, the craving for happiness led me by an imperceptible descent to love another woman and make a second home. And do not imagine that I am singular; there are in this city thousands of husbands, all led by various causes to live this twofold life."

"Great God!" cried the Countess. "How heavy is the cross Thou hast laid on me to bear! If the husband Thou hast given me here below in Thy wrath can only be made happy through my death, take me to Thyself!"

"If you had always breathed such admirable sentiments and such devotion, we should be happy yet," said the Count coldly.

"Indeed," cried Angelique, melting into a flood of tears, "forgive me if I have done any wrong. Yes, monsieur, I am ready to obey you in all things, feeling sure that you will desire nothing but what is just and natural; henceforth I will be all you can wish your wife to be."

"If your purpose, madame, is to compel me to say that I no longer love you, I shall find the cruel courage to tell you so. Can I command my heart? Can I wipe out in an instant the traces of fifteen years of suffering?—I have ceased to love.—These words contain a mystery as deep as lies the words I love. Esteem, respect, friendship may be won, lost, regained; but as to love—I might school myself for a thousand years, and it would not blossom again, especially for a woman too old to respond to it."

"I hope, Monsieur le Comte, I sincerely hope, that such words may not be spoken to you some day by the woman you love, and in such a tone and accent—"

"Will you put on a dress a la Grecque this evening, and come to the Opera?"

The shudder with which the Countess received the suggestion was a mute reply.

Early in December 1833, a man, whose perfectly white hair and worn features seemed to show that he was aged by grief rather than by years, was walking at midnight along the Rue Gaillon. Having reached a house of modest appearance, and only two stories high, he paused to look up at one of the attic windows that pierced the roof at regular intervals. A dim light scarcely showed through the humble panes, some of which had been repaired with paper. The man below was watching the wavering glimmer with the vague curiosity of a Paris idler, when a young man came out of the house. As the light of the street lamp fell full on the face of the first comer, it will not seem surprising that, in spite of the darkness, this young man went towards the passer-by, though with the hesitancy that is usual when we have any fear of making a mistake in recognizing an acquaintance.

"What, is it you," cried he, "Monsieur le President? Alone at this hour, and so far from the Rue Saint-Lazare. Allow me to have the honor of giving you my arm.—The pavement is so greasy this morning, that if we do not hold each other up," he added, to soothe the elder man's susceptibilities, "we shall find it hard to escape a tumble."

"But, my dear sir, I am no more than fifty-five, unfortunately for me," replied the Comte de Granville. "A physician of your celebrity must know that at that age a man is still hale and strong."

"Then you are in waiting on a lady, I suppose," replied Horace Bianchon. "You are not, I imagine, in the habit of going about Paris on foot. When a man keeps such fine horses——"

"Still, when I am not visiting in the evening, I commonly return from the Courts or the club on foot," replied the Count.

"And with large sums of money about you, perhaps!" cried the doctor. "It is a positive invitation to the assassin's knife."

"I am not afraid of that," said Granville, with melancholy indifference.

"But, at least, do not stand about," said the doctor, leading the Count towards the boulevard. "A little more and I shall believe that you are bent of robbing me of your last illness, and dying by some other hand than mine."

"You caught me playing the spy," said the Count. "Whether on foot or in a carriage, and at whatever hour of the night I may come by, I have for some time past observed at a window on the third floor of your house the shadow of a person who seems to work with heroic constancy."

The Count paused as if he felt some sudden pain. "And I take as great an interest in that garret," he went on, "as a citizen of Paris must feel in the finishing of the Palais Royal."

"Well," said Horace Bianchon eagerly, "I can tell you—"

"Tell me nothing," replied Granville, cutting the doctor short. "I would not give a centime to know whether the shadow that moves across that shabby blind is that of a man or a woman, nor whether the inhabitant of that attic is happy or miserable. Though I was surprised to see no one at work there this evening, and though I stopped to look, it was solely for the pleasure of indulging in conjectures as numerous and as idiotic as those of idlers who see a building left half finished. For nine years, my young—" the Count hesitated to use a word; then he waved his hand, exclaiming—"No, I will not say friend—I hate everything that savors of sentiment.— Well, for nine years past I have ceased to wonder that old men amuse themselves with growing flowers and planting trees; the events of life have taught them disbelief in all human affection; and I grew old within a few days. I will no longer attach myself to any creature but to unreasoning animals, or plants, or superficial things. I think more of Taglioni's grace than of all human feeling. I abhor life and the world in which I live alone. Nothing, nothing," he went on, in a tone that startled the younger man, "no, nothing can move or interest me."

"But you have children?"

"My children!" he repeated bitterly. "Yes—well, is not my eldest daughter the Comtesse de Vandenesse? The other will, through her sister's connections, make some good match. As to my sons, have they not succeeded? The Viscount was public prosecutor at Limoges, and is now President of the Court at Orleans; the younger is public prosecutor in Paris.—My children have their own cares, their own anxieties and business to attend to. If of all those hearts one had been devoted to me, if one had tried by entire affection to fill up the void I have here," and he struck his breast, "well, that one would have failed in life, have sacrificed it to me. And why should he? Why? To bring sunshine into my few remaining years—and would he have succeeded? Might I not have accepted such generosity as a debt? But, doctor," and the Count smiled with deep irony, "it is not for nothing that we teach them arithmetic and how to count. At this moment perhaps they are waiting for my money."

"O Monsieur le Comte, how could such an idea enter your head—you who are kind, friendly, and humane! Indeed, if I were not myself a living proof of the benevolence you exercise so liberally and so nobly—"

"To please myself," replied the Count. "I pay for a sensation, as I would to-morrow pay a pile of gold to recover the most childish illusion that would but make my heart glow.—I help my fellow-creatures for my own sake, just as I gamble; and I look for gratitude from none. I should see you die without blinking; and I beg of you to feel the same with regard to me. I tell you, young man, the events of life have swept over my heart like the lavas of Vesuvius over Herculaneum. The town is there—dead."

"Those who have brought a soul as warm and as living as yours was to such a pitch of indifference are indeed guilty!"

"Say no more," said the Count, with a shudder of aversion.

"You have a malady which you ought to allow me to treat," said Bianchon in a tone of deep emotion.

"What, do you know of a cure for death?" cried the Count irritably.

"I undertake, Monsieur le Comte, to revive the heart you believe to be frozen."

"Are you a match for Talma, then?" asked the Count satirically.

"No, Monsieur le Comte. But Nature is as far above Talma as Talma is superior to me.—Listen: the garret you are interested in is inhabited by a woman of about thirty, and in her love is carried to fanaticism. The object of her adoration is a young man of pleasing appearance but endowed by some malignant fairy with every conceivable vice. This fellow is a gambler, and it is hard to say which he is most addicted to—wine or women; he has, to my knowledge, committed acts deserving punishment by law. Well, and to him this unhappy woman sacrificed a life of ease, a man who worshiped her, and the father of her children.—But what is wrong, Monsieur le Comte?"

"Nothing. Go on."

"She has allowed him to squander a perfect fortune; she would, I believe, give him the world if she had it; she works night and day; and many a time she has, without a murmur, seen the wretch she adores rob her even of the money saved to buy the clothes the children need, and their food for the morrow. Only three days ago she sold her hair, the finest hair I ever saw; he came in, she could not hide the gold piece quickly enough, and he asked her for it. For a smile, for a kiss, she gave up the price of a fortnight's life and peace. Is it not dreadful, and yet sublime?—But work is wearing her cheeks hollow. Her children's crying has broken her heart; she is ill, and at this moment on her wretched bed. This evening they had nothing to eat; the children have not strength to cry, they were silent when I went up."

Horace Bianchon stood still. Just then the Comte de Granville, in spite of himself, as it were, had put his hand into his waistcoat pocket.

"I can guess, my young friend, how it is that she is yet alive if you attend her," said the elder man.

"O poor soul!" cried the doctor, "who could refuse to help her? I only wish I were richer, for I hope to cure her of her passion."

"But how can you expect me to pity a form of misery of which the joys to me would seem cheaply purchased with my whole fortune!" exclaimed the Count, taking his hand out of his pocket empty of the notes which Bianchon had supposed his patron to be feeling for. "That woman feels, she is alive! Would not Louis XV. have given his kingdom to rise from the grave and have three days of youth and life! And is not that the history of thousands of dead men, thousands of sick men, thousands of old men?"

"Poor Caroline!" cried Bianchon.

As he heard the name the Count shuddered, and grasped the doctor's arm with the grip of an iron vise, as it seemed to Bianchon.

"Her name is Caroline Crochard?" asked the President, in a voice that was evidently broken.

"Then you know her?" said the doctor, astonished.

"And the wretch's name is Solvet.—Ay, you have kept your word!" exclaimed Granville; "you have roused my heart to the most terrible pain it can suffer till it is dust. That emotion, too, is a gift from hell, and I always know how to pay those debts."

By this time the Count and the doctor had reached the corner of the Rue de la Chaussee d'Antin. One of those night-birds who wonder round with a basket on their back and crook in hand, and were, during the Revolution, facetiously called the Committee of Research, was standing by the curbstone where the two men now stopped. This scavenger had a shriveled face worthy of those immortalized by Charlet in his caricatures of the sweepers of Paris.

"Do you ever pick up a thousand-franc note?"

"Now and then, master."

"And you restore them?"

"It depends on the reward offered."

"You're the man for me," cried the Count, giving the man a thousand-franc note. "Take this, but, remember, I give it to you on condition of your spending it at the wineshop, of your getting drunk, fighting, beating your wife, blacking your friends' eyes. That will give work to the watch, the surgeon, the druggist—perhaps to the police, the public prosecutor, the judge, and the prison warders. Do not try to do anything else, or the devil will be revenged on you sooner or later."

A draughtsman would need at once the pencil of Charlet and of Callot, the brush of Teniers and of Rembrandt, to give a true notion of this night-scene.

"Now I have squared accounts with hell, and had some pleasure for my money," said the Count in a deep voice, pointing out the indescribable physiognomy of the gaping scavenger to the doctor, who stood stupefied. "As for Caroline Crochard!—she may die of hunger and thirst, hearing the heartrending shrieks of her starving children, and convinced of the baseness of the man she loves. I will not give a sou to rescue her; and because you have helped her, I will see you no more——"

The Count left Bianchon standing like a statue, and walked as briskly as a young man to the Rue Saint-Lazare, soon reaching the little house where he resided, and where, to his surprise, he found a carriage waiting at the door.

"Monsieur, your son, the attorney-general, came about an hour since," said the man-servant, "and is waiting for you in your bedroom."

Granville signed to the man to leave him.

"What motive can be strong enough to require you to infringe the order I have given my children never to come to me unless I send for them?" asked the Count of his son as he went into the room.

"Father," replied the younger man in a tremulous voice, and with great respect, "I venture to hope that you will forgive me when you have heard me."

"Your reply is proper," said the Count. "Sit down," and he pointed to a chair, "But whether I walk up and down, or take a seat, speak without heeding me."

"Father," the son went on, "this afternoon, at four o'clock, a very young man who was arrested in the house of a friend of mine, whom he had robbed to a considerable extent, appealed to you.— He says he is your son."

"His name?" asked the Count hoarsely.

"Charles Crochard."

"That will do," said the father, with an imperious wave of the hand.

Granville paced the room in solemn silence, and his son took care not to break it.

"My son," he began, and the words were pronounced in a voice so mild and fatherly, that the young lawyer started, "Charles Crochard spoke the truth.—I am glad you came to me to-night, my good Eugene," he added. "Here is a considerable sum of money"—and he gave him a bundle of banknotes—"you can make any use of them you think proper in this matter. I trust you implicitly, and approve beforehand whatever arrangements you may make, either in the present or for the future.—Eugene my dear son, kiss me. We part perhaps for the last time. I shall to-morrow crave my dismissal from the King, and I am going to Italy.

"Though a father owes no account of his life to his children, he is bound to bequeath to them the experience Fate sells him so dearly—is it not a part of their inheritance?—When you marry," the count went on, with a little involuntary shudder, "do not undertake it lightly; that act is the most important of all which society requires of us. Remember to study at your leisure the character of the woman who is to be your partner; but consult me too, I will judge of her myself. A lack of union between husband and wife, from whatever cause, leads to terrible misfortune; sooner or later we are always punished for contravening the social law.—But I will write to you on this subject from Florence. A father who has the honor of presiding over a supreme court of justice must not have to blush in the presence of his son. Good-bye."

PARIS, February 1830-January 1842

MAITRE CORNELIUS

DEDICATION

To Monsieur le Comte Georges Mniszech:

Some envious being may think on seeing this page illustrated by one of the most illustrious of Sarmatian names, that I am striving, as the goldsmiths do, to enhance a modern work with an ancient jewel,—a fancy of the fashions of the day,—but you and a few others, dear count, will know that I am only seeking to pay my debt to Talent, Memory, and Friendship.

CHAPTER I

A CHURCH SCENE OF THE FIFTEENTH CENTURY

In 1479, on All Saints' day, the moment at which this history begins, vespers were ending in the cathedral of Tours. The archbishop Helie de Bourdeilles was rising from his seat to give the benediction himself to the faithful. The sermon had been long; darkness had fallen during the service, and in certain parts of the noble church (the towers of which were not yet finished) the deepest obscurity prevailed. Nevertheless a goodly number of tapers were burning in honor of the saints on the triangular candle-trays destined to receive such pious offerings, the merit and signification of which have never been sufficiently explained. The lights on each altar and all the candelabra in the choir were burning. Irregularly shed among a forest of columns and arcades which supported the three naves of the cathedral, the gleam of these masses of candles barely lighted the immense building, because the strong shadows of the columns, projected among the galleries, produced fantastic forms which increased the darkness that already wrapped in gloom the arches, the vaulted ceilings, and the lateral chapels, always sombre, even at mid-day.

The crowd presented effects that were no less picturesque. Certain figures were so vaguely defined in the "chiaroscuro" that they seemed like phantoms; whereas others, standing in a full gleam of the scattered light, attracted attention like the principal heads in a picture. Some statues seemed animated, some men seemed petrified. Here and there eyes shone in the flutings of the columns, the floor reflected looks, the marbles spoke, the vaults re-echoed sighs, the edifice itself seemed endowed with life.

The existence of Peoples has no more solemn scenes, no

moments more majestic. To mankind in the mass, movement is needed to make it poetical; but in these hours of religious thought, when human riches unite themselves with celestial grandeur, incredible sublimities are felt in the silence; there is fear in the bended knee, hope in the clasping hands. The concert of feelings in which all souls are rising heavenward produces an inexplicable phenomenon of spirituality. The mystical exaltation of the faithful reacts upon each of them; the feebler are no doubt borne upward by the waves of this ocean of faith and love. Prayer, a power electrical, draws our nature above itself. This involuntary union of all wills, equally prostrate on the earth, equally risen into heaven, contains, no doubt, the secret of the magic influences wielded by the chants of the priests, the harmonies of the organ, the perfumes and the pomps of the altar, the voices of the crowd and its silent contemplations. Consequently, we need not be surprised to see in the middle-ages so many tender passions begun in churches after long ecstasies,—passions ending often in little sanctity, and for which women, as usual, were the ones to do penance. Religious sentiment certainly had, in those days, an affinity with love; it was either the motive or the end of it. Love was still a religion, with its fine fanaticism, its naive superstitions, its sublime devotions, which sympathized with those of Christianity.

The manners of that period will also serve to explain this alliance between religion and love. In the first place society had no meeting-place except before the altar. Lords and vassals, men and women were equals nowhere else. There alone could lovers see each other and communicate. The festivals of the Church were the theatre of former times; the soul of woman was more keenly stirred in a cathedral than it is at a ball or the opera in our day; and do not strong emotions invariably bring women back to love? By dint of mingling with life and grasping it in all its acts and interests, religion had made itself a sharer of all virtues, the accomplice of all vices. Religion had passed into science, into politics, into eloquence, into crimes, into the flesh of the sick man and the poor man; it mounted thrones; it was everywhere. These semi-learned observations will serve, perhaps, to vindicate the truth of this study, certain details of which may frighten the perfected morals of our age, which are, as everybody knows, a trifle straitlaced.

At the moment when the chanting ceased and the last notes of the organ, mingling with the vibrations of the loud "A-men" as it issued from the strong chests of the intoning clergy, sent a murmuring echo through the distant arches, and the hushed assembly were awaiting the beneficent words of the archbishop, a burgher, impatient to get home, or fearing for his purse in the tumult of the crowd when the worshippers dispersed, slipped quietly away, at the risk of being called a bad Catholic. On which, a nobleman, leaning against one of the enormous columns that surround the choir, hastened to take possession of the seat abandoned by the worthy Tourainean. Having done so, he quickly hid his face among the plumes of his tall gray cap, kneeling upon the chair with an air of contrition that even an inquisitor would have trusted.

Observing the new-comer attentively, his immediate neighbors seemed to recognize him; after which they returned to their prayers with a certain gesture by which they all expressed the same thought,—a caustic, jeering thought, a silent slander. Two old women shook their heads, and gave each other a glance that seemed to dive into futurity.

The chair into which the young man had slipped was close to a chapel placed between two columns and closed by an iron railing. It was customary for the chapter to lease at a handsome price to seignorial families, and even to rich burghers, the right to be present at the services, themselves and their servants exclusively, in the various lateral chapels of the long side-aisles of the cathedral. This simony is in practice to the present day. A woman had her chapel as she now has her opera-box. The families who hired these privileged places were required to decorate the altar of the chapel thus conceded to them, and each made it their pride to adorn their own sumptuously,—a vanity which the Church did not rebuke. In this particular chapel a lady was kneeling close to the railing on a handsome rug of red velvet with gold tassels, precisely opposite to the seat vacated of the burgher. A silver-gilt lamp, hanging from the vaulted ceiling of the chapel before an altar magnificently decorated, cast its pale light upon a prayer-book held by the lady. The book trembled violently in her hand when the young man approached her.

"A-men!"

To that response, sung in a sweet low voice which was painfully agitated, though happily lost in the general clamor, she added rapidly in a whisper:—

"You will ruin me."

The words were said in a tone of innocence which a man of any delicacy ought to have obeyed; they went to the heart and pierced it. But the stranger, carried away, no doubt, by one of those paroxysms of passion which stifle conscience, remained in his chair and raised his head slightly that he might look into the chapel.

"He sleeps!" he replied, in so low a voice that the words could be heard by the young woman only, as sound is heard in its echo.

The lady turned pale; her furtive glance left for a moment the vellum page of the prayer-book and turned to the old man whom the young man had designated. What terrible complicity was in that glance? When the young woman had cautiously examined the old seigneur, she drew a long breath and raised her forehead, adorned with a precious jewel, toward a picture of the Virgin; that simple movement, that attitude, the moistened glance, revealed her life with imprudent naivete; had she been wicked, she would certainly have dissimulated. The personage who thus alarmed the lovers was a little old man, hunchbacked, nearly bald, savage in expression, and wearing a long and discolored white beard cut in a fan-tail. The cross of Saint-Michel glittered on his breast; his coarse, strong hands, covered with gray hairs, which had been clasped, had now dropped slightly apart in the slumber to which he had imprudently yielded. The right hand seemed about to fall upon his dagger, the hilt of which was in the form of an iron shell. By the manner in which he had placed the weapon, this hilt was directly under his hand; if, unfortunately, the hand touched the iron, he would wake, no doubt, instantly, and glance at his wife. His sardonic lips, his pointed chin aggressively pushed forward, presented the characteristic signs of a malignant spirit, a sagacity coldly cruel, that would surely enable him to divine all because he suspected everything. His yellow forehead was wrinkled like those of men whose habit it is to believe nothing, to weigh all things, and who, like misers chinking their gold, search out the meaning and the value of human actions. His bodily frame, though deformed, was bony and solid, and seemed both vigorous and excitable; in short, you might have thought him a stunted ogre. Consequently, an inevitable danger awaited the young lady whenever this terrible seigneur woke. That jealous husband would surely not fail to see the difference between a worthy old burgher who gave him no umbrage, and the new-comer, young, slender, and elegant.

"Libera nos a malo," she said, endeavoring to make the young man comprehend her fears.

The latter raised his head and looked at her. Tears were in his eyes; tears of love and of despair. At sight of them the lady trembled and betrayed herself. Both had, no doubt, long resisted and could resist no longer a love increasing day by day through invincible obstacles, nurtured by terror, strengthened by youth. The lady was moderately handsome; but her pallid skin told of secret sufferings that made her interesting. She had, moreover, an elegant figure, and the finest hair in the world. Guarded by a tiger, she risked her life in whispering a word, accepting a look, and permitting a mere pressure of the hand. Love may never have been more deeply felt than in those hearts, never more delightfully enjoyed, but certainly no passion was ever more perilous. It was easy to divine that to these two beings air, sound, foot-falls, etc., things indifferent to other men, presented hidden qualities, peculiar properties which they distinguished. Perhaps their love made them find faithful interpreters in the icy hands of the old priest to whom they confessed their sins, and from whom they received the Host at the holy table. Love profound! love gashed into the soul like a scar upon the body which we carry through life! When these two young people looked at each other, the woman seemed to say to her lover, "Let us love each other and die!" To which the young knight answered, "Let us love each other and not die." In reply, she showed him a sign her old duenna and two pages. The duenna slept; the pages were young and seemingly careless of what might happen, either of good or evil, to their masters.

"Do not be frightened as you leave the church; let yourself be managed."

The young nobleman had scarcely said these words in a low voice, when the hand of the old seigneur dropped upon the hilt of his dagger. Feeling the cold iron he woke, and his yellow eyes fixed themselves instantly on his wife. By a privilege seldom granted even to men of genius, he awoke with his mind as clear, his ideas as lucid as though he had not slept at all. The man had the mania of jealousy. The lover, with one eye on his mistress, had watched the husband with the other, and he now rose quickly, effacing himself behind a column at the moment when the hand of the old man fell; after which he disappeared, swiftly as a bird. The lady lowered her eyes to her book and tried to seem calm; but she could not prevent her face from blushing and her heart from beating with unnatural violence. The old lord saw the unusual crimson on the cheeks, forehead, even the eyelids of his wife. He looked about him cautiously, but seeing no one to distrust, he said to his wife:—

"What are you thinking of, my dear?"

"The smell of the incense turns me sick," she replied.

"It is particularly bad to-day?" he asked.

In spite of this sarcastic query, the wily old man pretended to believe in this excuse; but he suspected some treachery and he resolved to watch his treasure more carefully than before.

The benediction was given. Without waiting for the end of the

"Soecula soeculorum," the crowd rushed like a torrent to the doors of the church. Following his usual custom, the old seigneur waited till the general hurry was over; after which he left his chapel, placing the duenna and the youngest page, carrying a lantern, before him; then he gave his arm to his wife and told the other page to follow them.

As he made his way to the lateral door which opened on the west side of the cloister, through which it was his custom to pass, a stream of persons detached itself from the flood which obstructed the great portals, and poured through the side aisle around the old lord and his party. The mass was too compact to allow him to retrace his steps, and he and his wife were therefore pushed onward to the door by the pressure of the multitude behind them. The husband tried to pass out first, dragging the lady by the arm, but at that instant he was pulled vigorously into the street, and his wife was torn from him by a stranger. The terrible hunchback saw at once that he had fallen into a trap that was cleverly prepared. Repenting himself for having slept, he collected his whole strength, seized his wife once more by the sleeve of her gown, and strove with his other hand to cling to the gate of the church; but the ardor of love carried the day against jealous fury. The young man took his mistress round the waist, and carried her off so rapidly, with the strength of despair, that the brocaded stuff of silk and gold tore noisily apart, and the sleeve alone remained in the hand of the old man. A roar like that of a lion rose louder than the shouts of the multitude, and a terrible voice howled out the words:—

"To me, Poitiers! Servants of the Comte de Saint-Vallier, here! Help! help!"

And the Comte Aymar de Poitiers, sire de Saint-Vallier, attempted to draw his sword and clear a space around him. But he found himself surrounded and pressed upon by forty or fifty gentlemen whom it would be dangerous to wound. Several among them, especially those of the highest rank, answered him with jests as they dragged him along the cloisters.

With the rapidity of lightning the abductor carried the countess into an open chapel and seated her behind the confessional on a wooden bench. By the light of the tapers burning before the saint to whom the chapel was dedicated, they looked at each other for a moment in silence, clasping hands, and amazed at their own audacity. The countess had not the cruel courage to reproach the young man for the boldness to which they owed this perilous and only instant of happiness.

"Will you fly with me into the adjoining States?" said the young man, eagerly. "Two English horses are awaiting us close by, able to do thirty leagues at a stretch."

"Ah!" she cried, softly, "in what corner of the world could you hide a daughter of King Louis XI.?"

"True," replied the young man, silenced by a difficulty he had not foreseen.

"Why did you tear me from my husband?" she asked in a sort of terror.

"Alas!" said her lover, "I did not reckon on the trouble I should feel in being near you, in hearing you speak to me. I have made plans,—two or three plans,—and now that I see you all seems accomplished."

"But I am lost!" said the countess.

"We are saved!" the young man cried in the blind enthusiasm of his love. "Listen to me carefully!"

"This will cost me my life!" she said, letting the tears that rolled in her eyes flow down her cheeks. "The count will kill me,—to-night, perhaps! But go to the king; tell him the tortures that his daughter has endured these five years. He loved me well when I was little; he called me 'Marie-full-of-grace,' because I was ugly. Ah! if he knew the man to whom he gave me, his anger would be terrible. I have not dared complain, out of pity for the count.

Besides, how could I reach the king? My confessor himself is a spy of Saint-Vallier. That is why I have consented to this guilty meeting, to obtain a defender,—some one to tell the truth to the king. Can I rely on—Oh!" she cried, turning pale and interrupting herself, "here comes the page!"

The poor countess put her hands before her face as if to veil it.

"Fear nothing," said the young seigneur, "he is won! You can safely trust him; he belongs to me. When the count contrives to return for you he will warn us of his coming. In the confessional," he added, in a low voice, "is a priest, a friend of mine, who will tell him that he drew you for safety out of the crowd, and placed you under his own protection in this chapel. Therefore, everything is arranged to deceive him."

At these words the tears of the poor woman stopped, but an expression of sadness settled down on her face.

"No one can deceive him," she said. "To-night he will know all. Save me from his blows! Go to Plessis, see the king, tell him—" she hesitated; then, some dreadful recollection giving her courage to confess the secrets of her marriage, she added: "Yes, tell him that to master me the count bleeds me in both arms—to exhaust me. Tell him that my husband drags me about by the hair of my head. Say that I am a prisoner; that—"

Her heart swelled, sobs choked her throat, tears fell from her eyes. In her agitation she allowed the young man, who was muttering broken words, to kiss her hands.

"Poor darling! no one can speak to the king. Though my uncle is grand-master of his archers, I could not gain admission to Plessis. My dear lady! my beautiful sovereign! oh, how she has suffered! Marie, let yourself say but two words, or we are lost!"

"What will become of us?" she murmured. Then, seeing on the dark wall a picture of the Virgin, on which the light from the lamp was falling, she cried out:—

"Holy Mother of God, give us counsel!"

"To-night," said the young man, "I shall be with you in your room."

"How?" she asked naively.

They were in such great peril that their tenderest words were devoid of love.

"This evening," he replied, "I shall offer myself as apprentice to Maitre Cornelius, the king's silversmith. I have obtained a letter of recommendation to him which will make him receive me. His house is next to yours. Once under the roof of that old thief, I can soon find my way to your apartment by the help of a silken ladder."

"Oh!" she said, petrified with horror, "if you love me don't go to Maitre Cornelius."

"Ah!" he cried, pressing her to his heart with all the force of his youth, "you do indeed love me!"

"Yes," she said; "are you not my hope? You are a gentleman, and I confide to you my honor. Besides," she added, looking at him with dignity, "I am so unhappy that you would never betray my trust. But what is the good of all this? Go, let me die, sooner than that you should enter that house of Maitre Cornelius. Do you not know that all his apprentices—"

"Have been hanged," said the young man, laughing.

"Oh, don't go; you will be made the victim of some sorcery."

"I cannot pay too dearly for the joy of serving you," he said, with a look that made her drop her eyes.

"But my husband?" she said.

"Here is something to put him to sleep," replied her lover, drawing from his belt a little vial.

"Not for always?" said the countess, trembling.

For all answer the young seigneur made a gesture of horror.

"I would long ago have defied him to mortal combat if he were not so old," he said. "God preserve me from ridding you of him in any other way."

"Forgive me," said the countess, blushing. "I am cruelly punished for my sins. In a moment of despair I thought of killing him, and I feared you might have the same desire. My sorrow is great that I have never yet been able to confess that wicked thought; but I fear it would be repeated to him and he would avenge it. I have shamed you," she continued, distressed by his silence, "I deserve your blame."

And she broke the vial by flinging it on the floor violently.

"Do not come," she said, "my husband sleeps lightly; my duty is to wait for the help of Heaven—that will I do!"

She tried to leave the chapel.

"Ah!" cried the young man, "order me to do so and I will kill him. You will see me to-night."

"I was wise to destroy that drug," she said in a voice that was faint with the pleasure of finding herself so loved. "The fear of awakening my husband will save us from ourselves."

"I pledge you my life," said the young man, pressing her hand.

"If the king is willing, the pope can annul my marriage. We will then be united," she said, giving him a look that was full of delightful hopes.

"Monseigneur comes!" cried the page, rushing in.

Instantly the young nobleman, surprised at the short time he had gained with his mistress and wondering at the celerity of the count, snatched a kiss, which was not refused.

"To-night!" he said, slipping hastily from the chapel.

Thanks to the darkness, he reached the great portal safely, gliding from column to column in the long shadows which they cast athwart the nave. An old canon suddenly issued from the confessional, came to the side of the countess and closed the iron railing before which the page was marching gravely up and down with the air of a watchman.

A strong light now announced the coming of the count. Accompanied by several friends and by servants bearing torches, he hurried forward, a naked sword in hand. His gloomy eyes seemed to pierce the shadows and to rake even the darkest corners of the cathedral.

"Monseigneur, madame is there," said the page, going forward to meet him.

The Comte de Saint-Vallier found his wife kneeling on the steps of the alter, the old priest standing beside her and reading his breviary. At that sight the count shook the iron railing violently as if to give vent to his rage.

"What do you want here, with a drawn sword in a church?" asked the priest.

"Father, that is my husband," said the countess.

The priest took a key from his sleeve, and unlocked the railed door of the chapel. The count, almost in spite of himself, cast a look into the confessional, then he entered the chapel, and seemed to be listening attentively to the sounds in the cathedral.

"Monsieur," said his wife, "you owe many thanks to this venerable canon, who gave me a refuge here."

The count turned pale with anger; he dared not look at his friends, who had come there more to laugh at him than to help him. Then he answered curtly:

"Thank God, father, I shall find some way to repay you."

He took his wife by the arm and, without allowing her to finish her curtsey to the canon, he signed to his servants and left the church without a word to the others who had accompanied him. His silence had something savage and sullen about it. Impatient to reach his home and preoccupied in searching for means to discover the truth, he took his way through the tortuous streets which at that time separated the cathedral from the Chancellerie, a fine building recently erected by the Chancellor Juvenal des Ursins, on the site of an old fortification given by Charles VII. to that faithful servant as a reward for his glorious labors.

The count reached at last the rue du Murier, in which his dwelling, called the hotel de Poitiers, was situated. When his escort of servants had entered the courtyard and the heavy gates were closed, a deep silence fell on the narrow street, where other great seigneurs had their houses, for this new quarter of the town was near to Plessis, the usual residence of the king, to whom the courtiers, if sent for, could go in a moment. The last house in this street was also the last in the town. It belonged to Maitre Cornelius Hoogworst, an old Brabantian merchant, to whom King Louis XI. gave his utmost confidence in those financial transactions which his crafty policy induced him to undertake outside of his own kingdom.

Observing the outline of the houses occupied respectively by Maitre Cornelius and by the Comte de Poitiers, it was easy to believe that the same architect had built them both and destined them for the use of tyrants. Each was sinister in aspect, resembling a small fortress, and both could be well defended against an angry populace. Their corners were upheld by towers like those which lovers of antiquities remark in towns where the hammer of the iconoclast has not yet prevailed. The bays, which had little depth, gave a great power of resistance to the iron shutters of the windows and doors. The riots and the civil wars so frequent in those tumultuous times were ample justification for these precautions.

As six o'clock was striking from the great tower of the Abbey Saint-Martin, the lover of the hapless countess passed in front of the hotel de Poitiers and paused for a moment to listen to the sounds made in the lower hall by the servants of the count, who were supping. Casting a glance at the window of the room where he supposed his love to be, he continued his way to the adjoining house. All along his way, the young man had heard the joyous uproar of many feasts given throughout the town in honor of the day. The ill-joined shutters sent out streaks of light, the chimneys smoked, and the comforting odor of roasted meats pervaded the town. After the conclusion of the church services, the inhabitants were regaling themselves, with murmurs of satisfaction which fancy can picture better than words can paint. But at this particular spot a deep silence reigned, because in these two houses lived two passions which never rejoiced. Beyond them stretched the silent country. Beneath the shadow of the steeples of Saint-Martin, these two mute dwellings, separated from the others in the same street and standing at the crooked end of it, seemed afflicted with leprosy. The building opposite to them, the home of the criminals of the State, was also under a ban. A young man would be readily impressed by this sudden contrast. About to fling himself into an enterprise that was horribly hazardous, it is no wonder that the daring young seigneur stopped short before the house of the silversmith, and called to mind the many tales furnished by the life of Maitre Cornelius,—tales which caused such singular horror to the countess. At this period a man of war, and even a lover, trembled at the mere word "magic." Few indeed were the minds and the imaginations which disbelieved in occult facts and tales of the marvellous. The lover of the Comtesse de Saint-Vallier, one of the daughters whom Louis XI. had in Dauphine by Madame de Sassenage, however bold he might be in other respects, was likely to think twice before he finally entered the house of a so-called sorcerer.

The history of Maitre Cornelius Hoogworst will fully explain the security which the silversmith inspired in the Comte de Saint-Vallier, the terror of the countess, and the hesitation that now took possession of the lover. But, in order to make the readers of this nineteenth century understand how such commonplace events could be turned into anything supernatural, and to make them share the alarms of that olden time, it is necessary to interrupt the course of this narrative and cast a rapid glance on the preceding life and adventures of Maitre Cornelius.

CHAPTER II
THE TORCONNIER

Cornelius Hoogworst, one of the richest merchants in Ghent, having drawn upon himself the enmity of Charles, Duke of Burgundy, found refuge and protection at the court of Louis XI. The king was conscious of the advantages he could gain from a man connected with all the principal commercial houses of Flanders, Venice, and the Levant; he naturalized, ennobled, and flattered Maitre Cornelius; all of which was rarely done by Louis XI. The monarch pleased the Fleming as much as the Fleming pleased the monarch. Wily, distrustful, and miserly; equally politic, equally learned; superior, both of them, to their epoch; understanding each other marvellously; they discarded and resumed with equal facility, the one his conscience, the other his religion; they loved the same Virgin, one by conviction, the other by policy; in short, if we may believe the jealous tales of Olivier de Daim and Tristan, the king went to the house of the Fleming for those diversions with which King Louis XI. diverted himself. History has taken care to transmit to our knowledge the licentious tastes of a monarch who was not averse to debauchery. The old Fleming found, no doubt, both pleasure and profit in lending himself to the capricious pleasures of his royal client.

Cornelius had now lived nine years in the city of Tours. During those years extraordinary events had happened in his house, which had made him the object of general execration. On his first arrival, he had spent considerable sums in order to put the treasures he brought with him in safety. The strange inventions made for him secretly by the locksmiths of the town, the curious precautions taken in bringing those locksmiths to his house in a way to compel their silence, were long the subject of countless tales which enlivened the evening gatherings of the city. These singular artifices on the part of the old man made every one suppose him the possessor of Oriental riches. Consequently the narrators of that region—the home of the tale in France—built rooms full of gold and precious tones in the Fleming's house, not omitting to attribute all this fabulous wealth to compacts with Magic.

Maitre Cornelius had brought with him from Ghent two Flemish valets, an old woman, and a young apprentice; the latter, a youth with a gentle, pleasing face, served him as secretary, cashier, factotum, and courier. During the first year of his settlement in Tours, a robbery of considerable amount took place in his house, and judicial inquiry showed that the crime must have been committed by one of its inmates. The old miser had his two valets and the secretary put in prison. The young man was feeble and he died under the sufferings of the "question" protesting his innocence. The valets confessed the crime to escape torture; but when the judge required them to say where the stolen property could be found, they kept silence, were again put to the torture, judged, condemned, and hanged. On their way to the scaffold they declared themselves innocent, according to the custom of all persons about to be executed.

The city of Tours talked much of this singular affair; but the criminals were Flemish, and the interest felt in their unhappy fate soon evaporated. In those days wars and seditions furnished endless excitements, and the drama of each day eclipsed that of the night before. More grieved by the loss he had met with than by the death of his three servants, Maitre Cornelius lived alone in his house with the old Flemish woman, his sister. He obtained permission from the king to use state couriers for his private affairs, sold his mules to a muleteer of the neighborhood, and lived from that moment in the deepest solitude, seeing no one but the king, doing his business by means of Jews, who, shrewd calculators, served him well in order to gain his all-powerful protection.

Some time after this affair, the king himself procured for his old "torconnier" a young orphan in whom he took an interest. Louis XI. called Maitre Cornelius familiarly by that obsolete term, which, under the reign of Saint-Louis, meant a usurer, a collector of imposts, a man who pressed others by violent means. The epithet, "tortionnaire," which remains to this day in our legal phraseology, explains the old word torconnier, which we often find spelt "tortionneur." The poor young orphan devoted himself carefully to the affairs of the old Fleming, pleased him much, and was soon high in his good graces. During a winter's night, certain diamonds deposited with Maitre Cornelius by the King of England as security for a sum of a hundred thousand crowns were stolen, and suspicion, of course, fell on the orphan. Louis XI. was all the more severe because he had answered for the youth's fidelity. After a very brief and summary examination by the grand provost, the unfortunate secretary was hanged. After that no one dared for a long time to learn the arts of banking and exchange from Maitre Cornelius.

In course of time, however, two young men of the town, Touraineans,—men of honor, and eager to make their fortunes,—took service with the silversmith. Robberies coincided with the admission of the two young men into the house. The circumstances of these crimes, the manner in which they were perpetrated, showed plainly that the robbers had secret communication with its inmates. Become by this time more than ever suspicious and vindictive, the old Fleming laid the matter before Louis XI., who placed it in the hands of his grand provost. A trial was promptly had and promptly ended. The inhabitants of Tours blamed Tristan l'Hermite secretly for unseemly haste. Guilty or not guilty, the young Touraineans were looked upon as victims, and Cornelius as an executioner. The two families thus thrown into mourning were much respected; their complaints obtained a hearing, and little by little it came to be believed that all the victims whom the king's silversmith had sent to the scaffold were innocent. Some persons declared that the cruel miser imitated the king, and sought to put terror and gibbets between himself and his fellow-men; others said that he had never been robbed at all,—that these melancholy executions were the result of cool calculations, and that their real object was to relieve him of all fear for his treasure.

The first effect of these rumors was to isolate Maitre Cornelius. The Touraineans treated him like a leper, called him the "tortionnaire," and named his house Malemaison. If the Fleming had found strangers to the town bold enough to enter it, the inhabitants would have warned them against doing so. The most favorable opinion of Maitre Cornelius was that of persons who thought him merely baneful. Some he inspired with instinctive terror; others he impressed with the deep respect that most men feel for limitless power and money, while to a few he certainly possessed the attraction of mystery. His way of life, his countenance, and the favor of the king, justified all the tales of which he had now become the subject.

Cornelius travelled much in foreign lands after the death of his persecutor, the Duke of Burgundy; and during his absence the king caused his premises to be guarded by a detachment of his own Scottish guard. Such royal solicitude made the courtiers believe that the old miser had bequeathed his property to Louis XI. When at home, the torconnier went out but little; but the lords of the court paid him frequent visits. He lent them money rather liberally, though capricious in his manner of doing so. On certain days he refused to give them a penny; the next day he would offer them large sums,—always at high interest and on good security. A good Catholic, he went regularly to the services, always attending the earliest mass at Saint-Martin; and as he had purchased there, as elsewhere, a chapel in perpetuity, he was separated even in church from other Christians. A popular proverb of that day, long remembered in Tours, was the saying: "You passed in front of the Fleming; ill-luck will happen to you." Passing in front of the Fleming explained all sudden pains and evils, involuntary sadness, ill-turns of fortune among the Touraineans. Even at court most persons attributed to Cornelius that fatal influence which Italian, Spanish, and Asiatic superstition has called the "evil eye." Without the terrible power of Louis XI., which was stretched like a mantle over that house, the populace, on the slightest opportunity, would have demolished La Malemaison, that "evil house" in the rue du Murier. And yet Cornelius had been the first to plant mulberries in

Tours, and the Touraineans at that time regarded him as their good genius. Who shall reckon on popular favor!

A few seigneurs having met Maitre Cornelius on his journeys out of France were surprised at his friendliness and good-humor. At Tours he was gloomy and absorbed, yet always he returned there. Some inexplicable power brought him back to his dismal house in the rue du Murier. Like a snail, whose life is so firmly attached to its shell, he admitted to the king that he was never at ease except under the bolts and behind the vermiculated stones of his little bastille; yet he knew very well that whenever Louis XI. died, the place would be the most dangerous spot on earth for him.

"The devil is amusing himself at the expense of our crony, the torconnier," said Louis XI. to his barber, a few days before the festival of All-Saints. "He says he has been robbed again, but he can't hang anybody this time unless he hangs himself. The old vagabond came and asked me if, by chance, I had carried off a string of rubies he wanted to sell me. 'Pasques-Dieu! I don't steal what I can take,' I said to him."

"Was he frightened?" asked the barber.

"Misers are afraid of only one thing," replied the king. "My crony the torconnier knows very well that I shall not plunder him unless for good reason; otherwise I should be unjust, and I have never done anything but what is just and necessary."

"And yet that old brigand overcharges you," said the barber.

"You wish he did, don't you?" replied the king, with the malicious look at his barber.

"Ventre-Mahom, sire, the inheritance would be a fine one between you and the devil!"

"There, there!" said the king, "don't put bad ideas into my head. My crony is a more faithful man than those whose fortunes I have made—perhaps because he owes me nothing."

For the last two years Maitre Cornelius had lived entirely alone with his aged sister, who was thought a witch. A tailor in the neighborhood declared that he had often seen her at night, on the roof of the house, waiting for the hour of the witches' sabbath. This fact seemed the more extraordinary because it was known to be the miser's custom to lock up his sister at night in a bedroom with iron-barred windows.

As he grew older, Cornelius, constantly robbed, and always fearful of being duped by men, came to hate mankind, with the one exception of the king, whom he greatly respected. He fell into extreme misanthropy, but, like most misers, his passion for gold, the assimilation, as it were, of that metal with his own substance, became closer and closer, and age intensified it. His sister herself excited his suspicions, though she was perhaps more miserly, more rapacious than her brother whom she actually surpassed in penurious inventions. Their daily existence had something mysterious and problematical about it. The old woman rarely took bread from the baker; she appeared so seldom in the market, that the least credulous of the townspeople ended by attributing to these strange beings the knowledge of some secret for the maintenance of life. Those who dabbled in alchemy declared that Maitre Cornelius had the power of making gold. Men of science averred that he had found the Universal Panacea. According to many of the country-people to whom the townsfolk talked of him, Cornelius was a chimerical being, and many of them came into the town to look at his house out of mere curiosity.

The young seigneur whom we left in front of that house looked about him, first at the hotel de Poitiers, the home of his mistress, and then at the evil house. The moonbeams were creeping round their angles, and tinting with a mixture of light and shade the hollows and reliefs of the carvings. The caprices of this white light gave a sinister expression to both edifices; it seemed as if Nature herself encouraged the superstitions that hung about the miser's dwelling. The young man called to mind the many traditions which made Cornelius a personage both curious and formidable. Though quite decided through the violence of his love to enter that house, and stay there long enough to accomplish his design, he hesitated to take the final step, all the while aware that he should certainly take it. But where is the man who, in a crisis of his life, does not willingly listen to presentiments as he hangs above the precipice? A lover worthy of being loved, the young man feared to die before he had been received for love's sake by the countess.

This mental deliberation was so painfully interesting that he did not feel the cold wind as it whistled round the corner of the building, and chilled his legs. On entering that house, he must lay aside his name, as already he had laid aside the handsome garments of nobility. In case of mishap, he could not claim the privileges of his rank nor the protection of his friends without bringing hopeless ruin on the Comtesse de Saint-Vallier. If her husband suspected the nocturnal visit of a lover, he was capable of roasting her alive in an iron cage, or of killing her by degrees in the dungeons of a fortified castle. Looking down at the shabby clothing in which he had disguised himself, the young nobleman felt ashamed. His black leather belt, his stout shoes, his ribbed socks, his linsey-woolsey breeches, and his gray woollen doublet made him look like the clerk of some poverty-stricken justice. To a noble of the fifteenth century it was like death itself to play the part of a beggarly burgher, and renounce the privileges of his rank. But—to climb the roof of the house where his mistress wept; to descend the chimney, or creep along from gutter to gutter to the window of her room; to risk his life to kneel beside her on a silken cushion before a glowing fire, during the sleep of a dangerous husband, whose snores would double their joy; to defy both heaven and earth in snatching the boldest of all kisses; to say no word that would not lead to death or at least to sanguinary combat if overheard,—all these voluptuous images and romantic dangers decided the young man. However slight might be the guerdon of his enterprise, could he only kiss once more the hand of his lady, he still resolved to venture all, impelled by the chivalrous and passionate spirit of those days. He never supposed for a moment that the countess would refuse him the soft happiness of love in the midst of such mortal danger. The adventure was too perilous, too impossible not to be attempted and carried out.

Suddenly all the bells in the town rang out the curfew,—a custom fallen elsewhere into desuetude, but still observed in the provinces, where venerable habits are abolished slowly. Though the lights were not put out, the watchmen of each quarter stretched the chains across the streets. Many doors were locked; the steps of a few belated burghers, attended by their servants, armed to the teeth and bearing lanterns, echoed in the distance. Soon the town, garroted as it were, seemed to be asleep, and safe from robbers and evil-doers, except through the roofs. In those days the roofs of houses were much frequented after dark. The streets were so narrow in the provincial towns, and even in Paris, that robbers could jump from the roofs on one side to those on the other. This perilous occupation was long the amusement of King Charles IX. in his youth, if we may believe the memoirs of his day.

Fearing to present himself too late to the old silversmith, the young nobleman now went up to the door of the Malemaison intending to knock, when, on looking at it, his attention was excited by a sort of vision, which the writers of those days would have called "cornue,"—perhaps with reference to horns and hoofs. He rubbed his eyes to clear his sight, and a thousand diverse sentiments passed through his mind at the spectacle before him. On each side of the door was a face framed in a species of loophole. At first he took these two faces for grotesque masks carved in stone, so angular, distorted, projecting, motionless, discolored were they; but the cold air and the moonlight presently enabled him to distinguish the faint white mist which living breath sent from two purplish noses; then he saw in each hollow face, beneath the shadow of the eyebrows, two eyes of porcelain blue casting clear fire, like those of a wolf crouching in the brushwood as it hears the baying of the hounds. The uneasy gleam of those eyes was turned on him so fixedly that, after receiving it for fully a minute, during which he examined the singular sight, he felt like a bird at which a setter points; a feverish tumult rose in his soul, but he quickly repressed it. The two faces, strained and suspicious, were doubtless those of Cornelius and his sister.

The young man feigned to be looking about him to see where he was, and whether this were the house named on a card which he drew from his pocket and pretended to read in the moonlight; then he walked straight to the door and struck three blows upon it, which echoed within the house as if it were the entrance to a cave. A faint light crept beneath the threshold, and an eye appeared at a small and very strong iron grating.

"Who is there?"

"A friend, sent by Oosterlinck, of Brussels."

"What do you want?"

"To enter."

"Your name?"

"Philippe Goulenoire."

"Have you brought credentials?"

"Here they are."

"Pass them through the box."

"Where is it?"

"To your left."

Philippe Goulenoire put the letter through the slit of an iron box above which was a loophole.

"The devil!" thought he, "plainly the king comes here, as they say he does; he couldn't take more precautions at Plessis."

He waited for more than a quarter of an hour in the street. After that lapse of time, he heard Cornelius saying to his sister, "Close the traps of the door."

A clinking of chains resounded from within. Philippe heard the bolts run, the locks creak, and presently a small low door, iron-bound, opened to the slightest distance through which a man could pass. At the risk of tearing off his clothing, Philippe squeezed himself rather than walked into La Malemaison. A toothless old woman with a hatchet face, the eyebrows projecting like the handles of a cauldron, the nose and chin so near together that a nut could scarcely pass between them,—a pallid, haggard creature, her hollow temples composed apparently of only bones and nerves,—guided the "soi-disant" foreigner silently into a lower room, while Cornelius followed prudently behind him.

"Sit there," she said to Philippe, showing him a three-legged stool placed at the corner of a carved stone fireplace, where there was no fire.

On the other side of the chimney-piece was a walnut table with twisted legs, on which was an egg in a plate and ten or a dozen little bread-sops, hard and dry and cut with studied parsimony. Two stools placed beside the table, on one of which the old woman sat down, showed that the miserly pair were eating their suppers. Cornelius went to the door and pushed two iron shutters into their place, closing, no doubt, the loopholes through which they had been gazing into the street; then he returned to his seat. Philippe Goulenoire (so called) next beheld the brother and sister dipping their sops into the egg in turn, and with the utmost gravity and the same precision with which soldiers dip their spoons in regular rotation into the mess-pot. This performance was done in silence. But as he ate, Cornelius examined the false apprentice with as much care and scrutiny as if he were weighing an old coin.

Philippe, feeling that an icy mantle had descended on his shoulders, was tempted to look about him; but, with the circumspection dictated by all amorous enterprises, he was careful not to glance, even furtively, at the walls; for he fully understood that if Cornelius detected him, he would not allow so inquisitive a person to remain in his house. He contented himself, therefore, by looking first at the egg and then at the old woman, occasionally contemplating his future master.

Louis XI.'s silversmith resembled that monarch. He had even acquired the same gestures, as often happens where persons dwell together in a sort of intimacy. The thick eyebrows of the Fleming almost covered his eyes; but by raising them a little he could flash out a lucid, penetrating, powerful glance, the glance of men habituated to silence, and to whom the phenomenon of the concentration of inward forces has become familiar. His thin lips, vertically wrinkled, gave him an air of indescribable craftiness. The lower part of his face bore a vague resemblance to the muzzle of a fox, but his lofty, projecting forehead, with many lines, showed great and splendid qualities and a nobility of soul, the springs of which had been lowered by experience until the cruel teachings of life had driven it back into the farthest recesses of this most singular human being. He was certainly not an ordinary miser; and his passion covered, no doubt, extreme enjoyments and secret conceptions.

"What is the present rate of Venetian sequins?" he said abruptly to his future apprentice.

"Three-quarters at Brussels; one in Ghent."

"What is the freight on the Scheldt?"

"Three sous parisis."

"Any news at Ghent?"

"The brother of Lieven d'Herde is ruined."

"Ah!"

After giving vent to that exclamation, the old man covered his knee with the skirt of his dalmatian, a species of robe made of black velvet, open in front, with large sleeves and no collar, the sumptuous material being defaced and shiny. These remains of a magnificent costume, formerly worn by him as president of the tribunal of the Parchons, functions which had won him the enmity of the Duke of Burgundy, was now a mere rag.

Philippe was not cold; he perspired in his harness, dreading further questions. Until then the brief information obtained that morning from a Jew whose life he had formerly saved, had sufficed him, thanks to his good memory and the perfect knowledge the Jew possessed of the manners and habits of Maitre Cornelius. But the young man who, in the first flush of his enterprise, had feared nothing was beginning to perceive the difficulties it presented. The solemn gravity of the terrible Fleming reacted upon him. He felt himself under lock and key, and remembered how the grand provost Tristan and his rope were at the orders of Maitre Cornelius.

"Have you supped?" asked the silversmith, in a tone which signified, "You are not to sup."

The old maid trembled in spite of her brother's tone; she looked at the new inmate as if to gauge the capacity of the stomach she might have to fill, and said with a specious smile:—

"You have not stolen your name; your hair and moustache are as black as the devil's tail."

"I have supped," he said.

"Well then," replied the miser, "you can come back and see me to-morrow. I have done without an apprentice for some years. Besides, I wish to sleep upon the matter."

"Hey! by Saint-Bavon, monsieur, I am a Fleming; I don't know a soul in this place; the chains are up in the streets, and I shall be put in prison. However," he added, frightened at the eagerness he was showing in his words, "if it is your good pleasure, of course I will go."

The oath seemed to affect the old man singularly.

"Come, come, by Saint-Bavon indeed, you shall sleep here."

"But—" said his sister, alarmed.

"Silence," replied Cornelius. "In his letter Oosterlinck tells me he will answer for this young man. You know," he whispered in his sister's ear, "we have a hundred thousand francs belonging to Oosterlinck? That's a hostage, hey!"

"And suppose he steals those Bavarian jewels? Tiens, he looks more like a thief than a Fleming."

"Hush!" exclaimed the old man, listening attentively to some sound.

Both misers listened. A moment after the "Hush!" uttered by Cornelius, a noise produced by the steps of several men echoed in the distance on the other side of the moat of the town.

"It is the Plessis guard on their rounds," said the sister.

"Give me the key of the apprentice's room," said Cornelius.

The old woman made a gesture as if to take the lamp.

"Do you mean to leave us alone, without light?" cried Cornelius, in a meaning tone of voice. "At your age can't you see in the dark? It isn't difficult to find a key."

The sister understood the meaning hidden beneath these words and left the room. Looking at this singular creature as she walked towards the door, Philippe Goulenoire was able to hide from Cornelius the glance which he hastily cast about the room. It was wainscoted in oak to the chair-strip, and the walls above were hung with yellow leather stamped with black arabesques; but what struck the young man most was a match-lock pistol with its formidable trigger. This new and terrible weapon lay close to Cornelius.

"How do you expect to earn your living with me?" said the latter.

"I have but little money," replied Philippe, "but I know good tricks in business. If you will pay me a sou on every mark I earn for you, that will satisfy me."

"A sou! a sou!" echoed the miser; "why, that's a good deal!"

At this moment the old sibyl returned with the key.

"Come," said Cornelius to Philippe.

The pair went out beneath the portico and mounted a spiral stone staircase, the round well of which rose through a high turret, beside the hall in which they had been sitting. At the first floor up the young man paused.

"No, no," said Cornelius. "The devil! this nook is the place where the king takes his ease."

The architect had constructed the room given to the apprentice under the pointed roof of the tower in which the staircase wound. It was a little room, all of stone, cold and without ornament of any kind. The tower stood in the middle of the facade on the courtyard, which, like the courtyards of all provincial houses, was narrow and dark. At the farther end, through an iron railing, could be seen a wretched garden in which nothing grew but the mulberries which Cornelius had introduced. The young nobleman took note of all this through the loopholes on the spiral staircase, the moon casting, fortunately, a brilliant light. A cot, a stool, a mismatched pitcher and basin formed the entire furniture of the room. The light could enter only through square openings, placed at intervals in the outside wall of the tower, according, no doubt, to the exterior ornamentation.

"Here is your lodging," said Cornelius; "it is plain and solid and contains all that is needed for sleep. Good night! Do not leave this room as the others did."

After giving his apprentice a last look full of many meanings, Cornelius double-locked the door, took away the key and descended the staircase, leaving the young nobleman as much befooled as a bell-founder when on opening his mould he finds nothing. Alone, without light, seated on a stool, in a little garret from which so many of his predecessors had gone to the scaffold, the young fellow felt like a wild beast caught in a trap. He jumped upon the stool and raised himself to his full height in order to reach one of the little openings through which a faint light shone. Thence he saw the Loire, the beautiful slopes of Saint-Cyr, the gloomy marvels of Plessis, where lights were gleaming in the deep recesses of a few windows. Far in the distance lay the beautiful meadows of Touraine and the silvery stream of her river. Every point of this lovely nature had, at that moment, a mysterious grace; the windows, the waters, the roofs of the houses shone like diamonds in the trembling light of the moon. The soul of the young seigneur could not repress a sad and tender emotion.

"Suppose it is my last farewell!" he said to himself.

He stood there, feeling already the terrible emotions his adventure offered him, and yielding to the fears of a prisoner who, nevertheless, retains some glimmer of hope. His mistress illumined each difficulty. To him she was no longer a woman, but a supernatural being seen through the incense of his desires. A feeble cry, which he fancied came from the hotel de Poitiers, restored him to himself and to a sense of his true situation. Throwing himself on his pallet to reflect on his course, he heard a slight movement which echoed faintly from the spiral staircase. He listened attentively, and the whispered words, "He has gone to bed," said by the old woman, reached his ear. By an accident unknown probably to the architect, the slightest noise on the staircase sounded in the room of the apprentices, so that Philippe did not lose a single movement of the miser and his sister who were watching him. He undressed, lay down, pretended to sleep, and employed the time during which the pair remained on the staircase, in seeking means to get from his prison to the hotel de Poitiers.

About ten o'clock Cornelius and his sister, convinced that their new inmate was sleeping, retired to their rooms. The young man studied carefully the sounds they made in doing so, and thought he could recognize the position of their apartments; they must, he believed, occupy the whole second floor. Like all the houses of that period, this floor was next below the roof, from which its windows projected, adorned with spandrel tops that were richly sculptured. The roof itself was edged with a sort of balustrade, concealing the gutters for the rain water which gargoyles in the form of crocodile's heads discharged into the street. The young seigneur, after studying this topography as carefully as a cat, believed he could make his way from the tower to the roof, and thence to Madame de Vallier's by the gutters and the help of a gargoyle. But he did not count on the narrowness of the loopholes of the tower; it was impossible to pass through them. He then resolved to get out upon the roof of the house through the window of the staircase on the second floor. To accomplish this daring project he must leave his room, and Cornelius had carried off the key.

By way of precaution, the young man had brought with him, concealed under his clothes, one of those poignards formerly used to give the "coup de grace" in a duel when the vanquished adversary begged the victor to despatch him. This horrible weapon had on one side a blade sharpened like a razor, and on the other a blade that was toothed like a saw, but toothed in the reverse direction from that by which it would enter the body. The young man determined to use this latter blade to saw through the wood around the lock. Happily for him the staple of the lock was put on to the outside of the door by four stout screws. By the help of his dagger he managed, not without great difficulty, to unscrew and remove it altogether, carefully laying it aside and the four screws with it. By midnight he was free, and he went down the stairs without his shoes to reconnoitre the localities.

He was not a little astonished to find a door wide open which led down a corridor to several chambers, at the end of which corridor was a window opening on a depression caused by the junction of the roofs of the hotel de Poitiers and that of the

Malemaison which met there. Nothing could express his joy, unless it be the vow which he instantly made to the Blessed Virgin to found a mass in her honor in the celebrated parish church of the Escrignoles at Tours. After examining the tall broad chimneys of the hotel de Poitiers he returned upon his steps to fetch his dagger, when to his horror, he beheld a vivid light on the staircase and saw Maitre Cornelius himself in his dalmatian, carrying a lamp, his eyes open to their fullest extent and fixed upon the corridor, at the entrance of which he stood like a spectre.

"If I open the window and jump upon the roofs, he will hear me," thought the young man.

The terrible old miser advanced, like the hour of death to a criminal. In this extremity Philippe, instigated by love, recovered his presence of mind; he slipped into a doorway, pressing himself back into the angle of it, and awaited the old man. When Cornelius, holding his lamp in advance of him, came into line with the current of air which the young man could send from his lungs, the lamp was blown out. Cornelius muttered vague words and swore a Dutch oath; but he turned and retraced his steps. The young man then rushed to his room, caught up his dagger and returned to the blessed window, opened it softly and jumped upon the roof.

Once at liberty under the open sky, he felt weak, so happy was he. Perhaps the extreme agitation of his danger of the boldness of the enterprise caused his emotion; victory is often as perilous as battle. He leaned against the balustrade, quivering with joy and saying to himself:—

"By which chimney can I get to her?"

He looked at them all. With the instinct given by love, he went to all and felt them to discover in which there had been a fire. Having made up his mind on that point, the daring young fellow stuck his dagger securely in a joint between two stones, fastened a silken ladder to it, threw the ladder down the chimney and risked himself upon it, trusting to his good blade, and to the chance of not having mistaken his mistress's room. He knew not whether Saint-Vallier was asleep or awake, but one thing he was resolved upon, he would hold the countess in his arms if it cost the life of two men.

Presently his feet gently touched the warm embers; he bent more gently still and saw the countess seated in an armchair; and she saw him. Pale with joy and palpitating, the timid creature showed him, by the light of the lamp, Saint-Vallier lying in a bed about ten feet from her. We may well believe their burning silent kisses echoed only in their hearts.

CHAPTER III

THE ROBBERY OF THE JEWELS OF
THE DUKE OF BAVARIA

The next day, about nine in the morning, as Louis XI. was leaving his chapel after hearing mass, he found Maitre Cornelius on his path.

"Good luck to you, crony," he said, shoving up his cap in his hasty way.

"Sire, I would willingly pay a thousand gold crowns if I could have a moment's talk with you; I have found the thief who stole the rubies and all the jewels of the Duke of—"

"Let us hear about that," said Louis XI., going out into the courtyard of Plessis, followed by his silversmith, Coyctier his physician, Olivier de Daim, and the captain of his Scottish guard. "Tell me about it. Another man to hang for you! Hola, Tristan!"

The grand provost, who was walking up and down the courtyard, came with slow steps, like a dog who exhibits his fidelity. The group paused under a tree. The king sat down on a bench and the courtiers made a circle about him.

"Sire, a man who pretended to be a Fleming has got the better of me—" began Cornelius.

"He must be crafty indeed, that fellow!" exclaimed Louis, wagging his head.

"Oh, yes!" replied the silversmith, bitterly. "But methinks he'd have snared you yourself. How could I distrust a beggar recommended to me by Oosterlinck, one hundred thousand francs of whose money I hold in my hands. I will wager the Jew's letter and seal were forged! In short, sire, I found myself this morning robbed of those jewels you admired so much. They have been ravished from me, sire! To steal the jewels of the Elector of Bavaria! those scoundrels respect nothing! they'll steal your kingdom if you don't take care. As soon as I missed the jewels I went up to the room of that apprentice, who is, assuredly, a past-master in thieving. This time we don't lack proof. He had forced the lock of his door. But when he got back to his room, the moon was down and he couldn't find all the screws. Happily, I felt one under my feet when I entered the room. He was sound asleep, the beggar, tired out. Just fancy, gentlemen, he got down into my strong-room by the chimney. To-morrow, or to-night, rather, I'll roast him alive. He had a silk ladder, and his clothes were covered with marks of his clambering over the roof and down the chimney. He meant to stay with me, and ruin me, night after night, the bold wretch! But where are the jewels? The country-folks coming into town early saw him on the roof. He must have had accomplices, who waited for him by that embankment you have been making. Ah, sire, you are the accomplice of fellows who come in boats; crack! they get off with everything, and leave no traces! But we hold this fellow as a key, the bold scoundrel! ah! a fine morsel he'll be for the gallows. With a little bit of questioning beforehand, we shall know all. Why, the glory of your reign is concerned in it! there ought not to be robbers in the land under so great a king."

The king was not listening. He had fallen into one of those gloomy meditations which became so frequent during the last years of his life. A deep silence reigned.

"This is your business," he said at length to Tristan; "take you hold of it."

He rose, walked a few steps away, and the courtiers left him alone. Presently he saw Cornelius, mounted on his mule, riding away in company with the grand provost.

"Where are those thousand gold crowns?" he called to him.

"Ah! sire, you are too great a king! there is no sum that can pay for your justice."

Louis XI. smiled. The courtiers envied the frank speech and privileges of the old silversmith, who promptly disappeared down the avenue of young mulberries which led from Tours to Plessis.

Exhausted with fatigue, the young seigneur had indeed fallen soundly asleep. Returning from his gallant adventure, he no longer felt the same ardor and courage to defend himself against distant or imaginary dangers with which he had rushed into the perils of the night. He had even postponed till the morrow the cleaning of his soiled garments; a great blunder, in which all else conspired. It was true that, lacking the moonlight, he had missed finding all the screws of that cursed lock; he had no patience to look for them. With the "laisser-aller" of a tired man, he trusted to his luck, which had so far served him well. He did, however, make a sort of compact with himself to awake at daybreak, but the events of the day and the agitations of the night did not allow him to keep faith with himself. Happiness is forgetful. Cornelius no longer seemed formidable to the young man when he threw himself on the pallet where so many poor wretches had wakened to their doom; and this light-hearted heedlessness proved his ruin. While the king's silversmith rode back from Plessis, accompanied by the grand provost and his redoubtable archers. The false Goulenoire was being watched by the old sister, seated on the corkscrew staircase oblivious of the cold, and knitting socks for Cornelius.

The young man continued to dream of the secret delights of that charming night, ignorant of the danger that was galloping towards him. He saw himself on a cushion at the feet of the countess, his head on her knees in the ardor of his love; he listened to the story of her persecutions and the details of the count's tyranny; he grew pitiful over the poor lady, who was, in truth, the best-loved natural daughter of Louis XI. He promised her to go on the morrow and reveal her wrongs to that terrible father; everything, he assured her, should be settled as they wished, the marriage broken off, the husband banished,—and all this within reach of that husband's sword, of which they might both be the victims if the slightest noise awakened him. But in the young man's dream the gleam of the lamp, the flame of their eyes, the colors of the stuffs and the tapestries were more vivid, more of love was in the air, more fire about them, than there had been in the actual scene. The Marie of his sleep resisted far less than the living Marie those adoring looks, those tender entreaties, those adroit silences, those voluptuous solicitations, those false generosities, which render the first moments of a passion so completely ardent, and shed into the soul a fresh delirium at each new step in love.

Following the amorous jurisprudence of the period, Marie de Saint-Vallier granted to her lover all the superficial rights of the tender passion. She willingly allowed him to kiss her foot, her robe, her hands, her throat; she avowed her love, she accepted the devotion and life of her lover; she permitted him to die for her; she yielded to an intoxication which the sternness of her semi-chastity increased; but farther than that she would not go; and she made her deliverance the price of the highest rewards of his love. In those days, in order to dissolve a marriage it was necessary to go to Rome; to obtain the help of certain cardinals, and to appear before the sovereign pontiff in person armed with the approval of the king. Marie was firm in maintaining her liberty to love, that she might sacrifice it to him later. Nearly every woman in those days had sufficient power to establish her empire over the heart of a man in a way to make that passion the history of his whole life, the spring and principle of his highest resolutions. Women were a power in France; they were so many sovereigns; they had forms of noble pride; their lovers belonged to them far more than they gave themselves to their lovers; often their love cost blood, and to be their lover it was necessary to incur great dangers. But the Marie of his dream made small defence against the young seigneur's ardent entreaties. Which of the two was the reality? Did the false apprentice in his dream see the true woman? Had he seen in the hotel de Poitiers a lady masked in virtue? The question is difficult to decide; and the honor of women demands that it be left, as it were, in litigation.

At the moment when the Marie of the dream may have been about to forget her high dignity as mistress, the lover felt himself seized by an iron hand, and the sour voice of the grand provost said to him:—

"Come, midnight Christian, who seeks God on the roofs, wake up!"

The young man saw the black face of Tristan l'Hermite above him, and recognized his sardonic smile; then, on the steps of the corkscrew staircase, he saw Cornelius, his sister, and behind them the provost guard. At that sight, and observing the diabolical faces expressing either hatred or curiosity of persons whose business it was to hang others, the so-called Philippe Goulenoire sat up on his pallet and rubbed his eyes.

"Mort-Dieu!" he cried, seizing his dagger, which was under the pillow. "Now is the time to play our knives."

"Ho, ho!" cried Tristan, "that's the speech of a noble. Methinks I see Georges d'Estouteville, the nephew of the grand master of the archers."

Hearing his real name uttered by Tristan, young d'Estouteville thought less of himself than of the dangers his recognition would bring upon his unfortunate mistress. To avert suspicion he cried out:—

"Ventre-Mahom! help, help to me, comrades!"

After that outcry, made by a man who was really in despair, the young courtier gave a bound, dagger in hand, and reached the landing. But the myrmidons of the grand provost were accustomed to such proceedings. When Georges d'Estouteville reached the stairs they seized him dexterously, not surprised by the vigorous thrust he made at them with his dagger, the blade of which fortunately slipped on the corselet of a guard; then, having disarmed him, they bound his hands, and threw him on the pallet before their leader, who stood motionless and thoughtful.

Tristan looked silently at the prisoner's hands, then he said to Cornelius, pointing to them:—

"Those are not the hands of a beggar, nor of an apprentice. He is a noble."

"Say a thief!" cried the torconnier. "My good Tristan, noble or serf, he has ruined me, the villain! I want to see his feet warmed in your pretty boots. He is, I don't doubt it, the leader of that gang of devils, visible and invisible, who know all my secrets, open my locks, rob me, murder me! They have grown rich out of me, Tristan. Ha! this time we shall get back the treasure, for the fellow has the face of the king of Egypt. I shall recover my dear rubies, and all the sums I have lost; and our worthy king shall have his share in the harvest."

"Oh, our hiding-places are much more secure than yours!" said Georges, smiling.

"Ha! the damned thief, he confesses!" cried the miser.

The grand provost was engaged in attentively examining Georges d'Estouteville's clothes and the lock of the door.

"How did you get out those screws?"

Georges kept silence.

"Oh, very good, be silent if you choose. You will soon confess on the holy rack," said Tristan.

"That's what I call business!" cried Cornelius.

"Take him off," said the grand provost to the guards.

Georges d'Estouteville asked permission to dress himself. On a sign from their chief, the men put on his clothing with the clever rapidity of a nurse who profits by the momentary tranquillity of her nursling.

An immense crowd cumbered the rue du Murier. The growls

of the populace kept increasing, and seemed the precursors of a riot. From early morning the news of the robbery had spread through the town. On all sides the "apprentice," said to be young and handsome, had awakened public sympathy, and revived the hatred felt against Cornelius; so that there was not a young man in the town, nor a young woman with a fresh face and pretty feet to exhibit, who was not determined to see the victim. When Georges issued from the house, led by one of the provost's guard, who, after he had mounted his horse, kept the strong leathern thong that bound the prisoner tightly twisted round his arm, a horrible uproar arose. Whether the populace merely wished to see this new victim, or whether it intended to rescue him, certain it is that those behind pressed those in front upon the little squad of cavalry posted around the Malemaison. At this moment, Cornelius, aided by his sister, closed the door, and slammed the iron shutters with the violence of panic terror. Tristan, who was not accustomed to respect the populace of those days (inasmuch as they were not yet the sovereign people), cared little for a probable riot.

"Push on! push on!" he said to his men.

At the voice of their leader the archers spurred their horses towards the end of the street. The crowd, seeing one or two of their number knocked down by the horses and trampled on, and some others pressed against the sides of the horses and nearly suffocated, took the wiser course of retreating to their homes.

"Make room for the king's justice!" cried Tristan. "What are you doing here? Do you want to be hanged too? Go home, my friends, go home; your dinner is getting burnt. Hey! my good woman, go and darn your husband's stockings; get back to your needles."

Though such speeches showed that the grand provost was in good humor, they made the most obstreperous fly as if he were flinging the plague upon them.

At the moment when the first movement of the crowd took

place, Georges d'Estouteville was stupefied at seeing, at one of the windows of the hotel de Poitiers, his dear Marie de Saint-Vallier, laughing with the count. She was mocking at him, poor devoted lover, who was going to his death for her. But perhaps she was only amused at seeing the caps of the populace carried off on the spears of the archers. We must be twenty-three years old, rich in illusions, able to believe in a woman's love, loving ourselves with all the forces of our being, risking our life with delight on the faith of a kiss, and then betrayed, to understand the fury of hatred and despair which took possession of Georges d'Estouteville's heart at the sight of his laughing mistress, from whom he received a cold and indifferent glance. No doubt she had been there some time; she was leaning from the window with her arms on a cushion; she was at her ease, and her old man seemed content. He, too, was laughing, the cursed hunchback! A few tears escaped the eyes of the young man; but when Marie de Saint-Vallier saw them she turned hastily away. Those tears were suddenly dried, however, when Georges beheld the red and white plumes of the page who was devoted to his interests. The count took no notice of this servitor, who advanced to his mistress on tiptoe. After the page had said a few words in her ear, Marie returned to the window. Escaping for a moment the perpetual watchfulness of her tyrant, she cast one glance upon Georges that was brilliant with the fires of love and hope, seeming to say:—

"I am watching over you."

Had she cried the words aloud, she could not have expressed their meaning more plainly than in that glance, full of a thousand thoughts, in which terror, hope, pleasure, the dangers of their mutual situation all took part. He had passed, in that one moment, from heaven to martyrdom and from martyrdom back to heaven! So then, the brave young seigneur, light-hearted and content, walked gaily to his doom; thinking that the horrors of the "question" were not sufficient payment for the delights of his love.

As Tristan was about leaving the rue du Murier, his people

stopped him, seeing an officer of the Scottish guard riding towards them at full speed.

"What is it?" asked the provost.

"Nothing that concerns you," replied the officer, disdainfully. "The king has sent me to fetch the Comte and Comtesse de Saint-Vallier, whom he invites to dinner."

The grand provost had scarcely reached the embankment leading to Plessis, when the count and his wife, both mounted, she on her white mule, he on his horse, and followed by two pages, joined the archers, in order to enter Plessis-lez-Tours in company. All were moving slowly. Georges was on foot, between two guards on horseback, one of whom held him still by the leathern thong. Tristan, the count, and his wife were naturally in advance; the criminal followed them. Mingling with the archers, the young page questioned them, speaking sometimes to the prisoner, so that he adroitly managed to say to him in a low voice:—

"I jumped the garden wall and took a letter to Plessis from madame to the king. She came near dying when she heard of the accusation against you. Take courage. She is going now to speak to the king about you."

Love had already given strength and wiliness to the countess. Her laughter was part of the heroism which women display in the great crises of life.

In spite of the singular fancy which possessed the author of "Quentin Durward" to place the royal castle of Plessis-lez-Tours upon a height, we must content ourselves by leaving it where it really was, namely on low land, protected on either side by the Cher and the Loire; also by the canal Sainte-Anne, so named by Louis XI. in honor of his beloved daughter, Madame de Beaujeu. By uniting the two rivers between the city of Tours and Plessis this canal not only served as a formidable protection to the castle, but it offered a most precious road to commerce. On the side towards Brehemont, a vast and fertile plain, the park was defended by a moat, the remains of which still show its enormous breadth and depth. At a period when the power of artillery was still in embryo, the position of Plessis, long since chosen by Louis XI. for his favorite retreat, might be considered impregnable. The castle, built of brick and stone, had nothing remarkable about it; but it was surrounded by noble trees, and from its windows could be seen, through vistas cut in the park (plexitium), the finest points of view in the world. No rival mansion rose near this solitary castle, standing in the very centre of the little plain reserved for the king and guarded by four streams of water.

If we may believe tradition, Louis XI. occupied the west wing, and from his chamber he could see, at a glance the course of the Loire, the opposite bank of the river, the pretty valley which the Croisille waters, and part of the slopes of Saint-Cyr. Also, from the windows that opened on the courtyard, he saw the entrance to his fortress and the embankment by which he had connected his favorite residence with the city of Tours. If Louis XI. had bestowed upon the building of his castle the luxury of architecture which Francois I. displayed afterwards at Chambord, the dwelling of the kings of France would ever have remained in Touraine. It is enough to see this splendid position and its magical effects to be convinced of its superiority over the sites of all other royal residences.

Louis XI., now in the fifty-seventh year of his age, had scarcely more than three years longer to live; already he felt the coming on of death in the attacks of his mortal malady. Delivered from his enemies; on the point of increasing the territory of France by the possessions of the Dukes of Burgundy through the marriage of the Dauphin with Marguerite, heiress of Burgundy (brought about by means of Desquerdes, commander of his troops in Flanders); having established his authority everywhere, and now meditating ameliorations in his kingdom of all kinds, he saw time slipping past him rapidly with no further troubles than those of old age. Deceived by every one, even by the minions about him, experience had intensified his natural distrust. The desire to live became in him the egotism of a king who has incarnated himself in his people; he wished to prolong his life in order to carry out his vast designs.

All that the common-sense of publicists and the genius of revolutions has since introduced of change in the character of monarchy, Louis XI. had thought of and devised. Unity of taxation, equality of subjects before the law (the prince being then the law) were the objects of his bold endeavors. On All-Saints' eve he had gathered together the learned goldsmiths of his kingdom for the purpose of establishing in France a unity of weights and measures, as he had already established the unity of power. Thus, his vast spirit hovered like an eagle over his empire, joining in a singular manner the prudence of a king to the natural idiosyncracies of a man of lofty aims. At no period in our history has the great figure of Monarchy been finer or more poetic. Amazing assemblages of contrasts! a great power in a feeble body; a spirit unbelieving as to all things here below, devoutly believing in the practices of religion; a man struggling with two powers greater than his own—the present and the future; the future in which he feared eternal punishment, a fear which led him to make so many sacrifices to the Church; the present, namely his life itself, for the saving of which he blindly obeyed Coyctier. This king, who crushed down all about him, was himself crushed down by remorse, and by disease in the midst of the great poem of defiant monarchy in which all power was concentrated. It was once more the gigantic and ever magnificent combat of Man in the highest manifestation of his forces tilting against Nature.

While awaiting his dinner, a repast which was taken in those days between eleven o'clock and mid-day, Louis XI., returning from a short promenade, sat down in a huge tapestried chair near the fireplace in his chamber. Olivier de Daim, and his doctor, Coyctier, looked at each other without a word, standing in the recess of a window and watching their master, who presently seemed asleep. The only sound that was heard were the steps of the two chamberlains on service, the Sire de Montresor, and Jean Dufou, Sire de Montbazon, who were walking up and down the adjoining hall. These two Tourainean seigneurs looked at the captain of the Scottish guard, who was sleeping in his chair, according to his usual custom. The king himself appeared to be dozing. His head had drooped upon his breast; his cap, pulled forward on his forehead, hid his eyes. Thus seated in his high chair, surmounted by the royal crown, he seemed crouched together like a man who had fallen asleep in the midst of some deep meditation.

At this moment Tristan and his cortege crossed the canal by the bridge of Sainte-Anne, about two hundred feet from the entrance to Plessis.

"Who is that?" said the king.

The two courtiers questioned each other with a look of surprise.

"He is dreaming," said Coyctier, in a low voice.

"Pasques-Dieu!" cried Louis XI., "do you think me mad? People are crossing the bridge. It is true I am near the chimney, and I may hear sounds more easily than you. That effect of nature might be utilized," he added thoughtfully.

"What a man!" said de Daim.

Louis XI. rose and went toward one of the windows that looked on the town. He saw the grand provost, and exclaimed:—

"Ha, ha! here's my crony and his thief. And here comes my little Marie de Saint-Vallier; I'd forgotten all about it. Olivier," he said, addressing the barber, "go and tell Monsieur de Montbazon to serve some good Bourgeuil wine at dinner, and see that the cook doesn't forget the lampreys; Madame le comtesse likes both those things. Can I eat lampreys?" he added, after a pause, looking anxiously at Coyctier.

For all answer the physician began to examine his master's face. The two men were a picture in themselves.

121

History and romance-writers have consecrated the brown camlet coat, and the breeches of the same stuff, worn by Louis XI. His cap, decorated with leaden medallions, and his collar of the order of Saint-Michel, are not less celebrated; but no writer, no painter has represented the face of that terrible monarch in his last years,—a sickly, hollow, yellow and brown face, all the features of which expressed a sour craftiness, a cold sarcasm. In that mask was the forehead of a great man, a brow furrowed with wrinkles, and weighty with high thoughts; but in his cheeks and on his lips there was something indescribably vulgar and common. Looking at certain details of that countenance you would have thought him a debauched husbandman, or a miserly peddler; and yet, above these vague resemblances and the decrepitude of a dying old man, the king, the man of power, rose supreme. His eyes, of a light yellow, seemed at first sight extinct; but a spark of courage and of anger lurked there, and at the slightest touch it could burst into flames and cast fire about him. The doctor was a stout burgher, with a florid face, dressed in black, peremptory, greedy of gain, and self-important. These two personages were framed, as it were, in that panelled chamber, hung with high-warped tapestries of Flanders, the ceiling of which, made of carved beams, was blackened by smoke. The furniture, the bed, all inlaid with arabesques in pewter, would seem to-day more precious than they were at that period when the arts were beginning to produce their choicest masterpieces.

"Lampreys are not good for you," replied the physician.

That title, recently substituted for the former term of "myrrh-master," is still applied to the faculty in England. The name was at this period given to doctors everywhere.

"Then what may I eat?" asked the king, humbly.

"Salt mackerel. Otherwise, you have so much bile in motion that you may die on All-Souls' Day."

"To-day!" cried the king in terror.

"Compose yourself, sire," replied Coyctier. "I am here. Try not to fret your mind; find some way to amuse yourself."

"Ah!" said the king, "my daughter Marie used to succeed in that difficult business."

As he spoke, Imbert de Bastarnay, sire of Montresor and Bridore, rapped softly on the royal door. On receiving the king's permission he entered and announced the Comte and Comtesse de Saint-Vallier. Louis XI. made a sign. Marie appeared, followed by her old husband, who allowed her to pass in first.

"Good-day, my children," said the king.

"Sire," replied his daughter in a low voice, as she embraced him, "I want to speak to you in secret."

Louis XI. appeared not to have heard her. He turned to the door and called out in a hollow voice, "Hola, Dufou!"

Dufou, seigneur of Montbazon and grand cup-bearer of France, entered in haste.

"Go to the maitre d'hotel, and tell him I must have salt mackerel for dinner. And go to Madame de Beaujeu, and let her know that I wish to dine alone to-day. Do you know, madame," continued the king, pretending to be slightly angry, "that you neglect me? It is almost three years since I have seen you. Come, come here, my pretty," he added, sitting down and holding out his arms to her. "How thin you have grown! Why have you let her grow so thin?" said the king, roughly, addressing the Comte de Poitiers.

The jealous husband cast so frightened a look at his wife that she almost pitied him.

"Happiness, sire!" he stammered.

"Ah! you love each other too much,—is that it?" said the king, holding his daughter between his knees. "I did right to call you

Mary-full-of-grace. Coyctier, leave us! Now, then, what do you want of me?" he said to his daughter the moment the doctor had gone. "After sending me your—"

In this danger, Marie boldly put her hand on the king's lips and said in his ear,—

"I always thought you cautious and penetrating."

"Saint-Vallier," said the king, laughing, "I think that Bridore has something to say to you."

The count left the room; but he made a gesture with his shoulders well known to his wife, who could guess the thoughts of the jealous man, and knew she must forestall his cruel designs.

"Tell me, my child, how do you think I am,—hey? Do I seem changed to you?"

"Sire, do you want me to tell you the real truth, or would you rather I deceived you?"

"No," he said, in a low voice, "I want to know truly what to expect."

"In that case, I think you look very ill to-day; but you will not let my truthfulness injure the success of my cause, will you?"

"What is your cause?" asked the king, frowning and passing a hand across his forehead.

"Ah, sire," she replied, "the young man you have had arrested for robbing your silversmith Cornelius, and who is now in the hands of the grand provost, is innocent of the robbery."

"How do you know that?" asked the king. Marie lowered her head and blushed.

"I need not ask if there is love in this business," said the king, raising his daughter's head gently and stroking her chin. "If you don't confess every morning, my daughter, you will go to hell."

"Cannot you oblige me without forcing me to tell my secret thoughts?"

"Where would be the pleasure?" cried the king, seeing only an amusement in this affair.

"Ah! do you want your pleasure to cost me grief?"

"Oh! you sly little girl, haven't you any confidence in me?"

"Then, sire, set the young nobleman at liberty."

"So! he is a nobleman, is he?" cried the king. "Then he is not an apprentice?"

"He is certainly innocent," she said.

"I don't see it so," said the king, coldly. "I am the law and justice of my kingdom, and I must punish evil-doers."

"Come, don't put on that solemn face of yours! Give me the life of that young man."

"Is it yours already?"

"Sire," she said, "I am pure and virtuous. You are jesting at—"

"Then," said Louis XI., interrupting her, "as I am not to know the truth, I think Tristan had better clear it up."

Marie turned pale, but she made a violent effort and cried out:—

"Sire, I assure you, you will regret all this. The so-called thief stole nothing. If you will grant me his pardon, I will tell you everything, even though you may punish me."

"Ho, ho! this is getting serious," cried the king, shoving up his cap. "Speak out, my daughter."

"Well," she said, in a low voice, putting her lips to her father's ear, "he was in my room all night."

"He could be there, and yet rob Cornelius. Two robberies!"

"I have your blood in my veins, and I was not born to love a scoundrel. That young seigneur is the nephew of the captain-general of your archers."

"Well, well!" cried the king; "you are hard to confess."

With the words the king pushed his daughter from his knee, and hurried to the door of the room, but softly on tiptoe, making no noise. For the last moment or two, the light from a window in the adjoining hall, shining through a space below the door, had shown him the shadow of a listener's foot projected on the floor of his chamber. He opened the door abruptly, and surprised the Comte de Saint-Vallier eavesdropping.

"Pasques-Dieu!" he cried; "here's an audacity that deserves the axe."

"Sire," replied Saint-Vallier, haughtily, "I would prefer an axe at my throat to the ornament of marriage on my head."

"You may have both," said Louis XI. "None of you are safe from such infirmities, messieurs. Go into the farther hall. Conyngham," continued the king, addressing the captain of the guard, "you are asleep! Where is Monsieur de Bridore? Why do you let me be approached in this way? Pasques-Dieu! the lowest burgher in Tours is better served than I am."

After scolding thus, Louis re-entered his room; but he took care to draw the tapestried curtain, which made a second door, intended more to stifle the words of the king than the whistling of the harsh north wind.

"So, my daughter," he said, liking to play with her as a cat plays with a mouse, "Georges d'Estouteville was your lover last night?"

"Oh, no, sire!"

"No! Ah! by Saint-Carpion, he deserves to die. Did the scamp not think my daughter beautiful?"

"Oh! that is not it," she said. "He kissed my feet and hands with an ardor that might have touched the most virtuous of women. He loves me truly in all honor."

"Do you take me for Saint-Louis, and suppose I should believe such nonsense? A young fellow, made like him, to have risked his life just to kiss your little slippers or your sleeves! Tell that to others."

"But, sire, it is true. And he came for another purpose."

Having said these words, Marie felt that she had risked the life of her husband, for Louis instantly demanded:

"What purpose?"

The adventure amused him immensely. But he did not expect the strange confidences his daughter now made to him after stipulating for the pardon of her husband.

"Ho, ho, Monsieur de Saint-Vallier! So you dare to shed the royal blood!" cried the king, his eyes lighting with anger.

At this moment the bell of Plessis sounded the hour of the king's dinner. Leaning on the arm of his daughter, Louis XI. appeared with contracted brows on the threshold of his chamber, and found all his servitors in waiting. He cast an ambiguous look on the Comte de Saint-Vallier, thinking of the sentence he meant to pronounce upon him. The deep silence which reigned was presently broken by the steps of Tristan l'Hermite as he mounted the grand staircase. The grand provost entered the hall, and, advancing toward the king, said:—

"Sire, the affair is settled."

"What! is it all over?" said the king.

"Our man is in the hands of the monks. He confessed the theft after a touch of the 'question.'"

The countess gave a sign, and turned pale; she could not speak, but looked at the king. That look was observed by Saint-Vallier, who muttered in a low tone: "I am betrayed; that thief is an acquaintance of my wife."

"Silence!" cried the king. "Some one is here who will wear out my patience. Go at once and put a stop to the execution," he continued, addressing the grand provost. "You will answer with your own body for that of the criminal, my friend. This affair must be better sifted, and I reserve to myself the doing of it. Set the prisoner at liberty provisionally; I can always recover him; these robbers have retreats they frequent, lairs where they lurk. Let Cornelius know that I shall be at his house to-night to begin the inquiry myself. Monsieur de Saint-Vallier," said the king, looking fixedly at the count, "I know about you. All your blood could not pay for one drop of mine; do you hear me? By our Lady of Clery! you have committed crimes of lese-majesty. Did I give you such a pretty wife to make her pale and weakly? Go back to your own house, and make your preparations for a long journey."

The king stopped at these words from a habit of cruelty; then he added:—

"You will leave to-night to attend to my affairs with the government of Venice. You need be under no anxiety about your wife; I shall take charge of her at Plessis; she will certainly be safe here. Henceforth I shall watch over her with greater care than I have done since I married her to you."

Hearing these words, Marie silently pressed her father's arm as if to thank him for his mercy and goodness. As for Louis XI., he was laughing to himself in his sleeve.

CHAPTER IV
THE HIDDEN TREASURE

Louis XI. was fond of intervening in the affairs of his subjects, and he was always ready to mingle his royal majesty with the burgher life. This taste, severely blamed by some historians, was really only a passion for the "incognito," one of the greatest pleasures of princes,—a sort of momentary abdication, which enables them to put a little real life into their existence, made insipid by the lack of opposition. Louis XI., however, played the incognito openly. On these occasions he was always the good fellow, endeavoring to please the people of the middle classes, whom he made his allies against feudality. For some time past he had found no opportunity to "make himself populace" and espouse the domestic interests of some man "engarrie" (an old word still used in Tours, meaning engaged) in litigious affairs, so that he shouldered the anxieties of Maitre Cornelius eagerly, and also the secret sorrows of the Comtesse de Saint-Vallier. Several times during dinner he said to his daughter:—

"Who, think you, could have robbed my silversmith? The robberies now amount to over twelve hundred thousand crowns in eight years. Twelve hundred thousand crowns, messieurs!" he continued, looking at the seigneurs who were serving him. "Notre Dame! with a sum like that what absolutions could be bought in Rome! And I might, Pasques-Dieu! bank the Loire, or, better still, conquer Piedmont, a fine fortification ready-made for this kingdom."

When dinner was over, Louis XI. took his daughter, his doctor, and the grand provost, with an escort of soldiers, and rode to the hotel de Poitiers in Tours, where he found, as he expected, the Comte de Saint-Vallier awaiting his wife, perhaps to make away with her life.

"Monsieur," said the king, "I told you to start at once. Say farewell to your wife now, and go to the frontier; you will be accompanied by an escort of honor. As for your instructions and credentials, they will be in Venice before you get there."

Louis then gave the order—not without adding certain secret instructions—to a lieutenant of the Scottish guard to take a squad of men and accompany the ambassador to Venice. Saint-Vallier departed in haste, after giving his wife a cold kiss which he would fain have made deadly. Louis XI. then crossed over to the Malemaison, eager to begin the unravelling of the melancholy comedy, lasting now for eight years, in the house of his silversmith; flattering himself that, in his quality of king, he had enough penetration to discover the secret of the robberies. Cornelius did not see the arrival of the escort of his royal master without uneasiness.

"Are all those persons to take part in the inquiry?" he said to the king.

Louis XI. could not help smiling as he saw the fright of the miser and his sister.

"No, my old crony," he said; "don't worry yourself. They will sup at Plessis, and you and I alone will make the investigation. I am so good in detecting criminals, that I will wager you ten thousand crowns I shall do so now."

"Find him, sire, and make no wager."

They went at once into the strong room, where the Fleming kept his treasure. There Louis, who asked to see, in the first place, the casket from which the jewels of the Duke of Burgundy had been taken, then the chimney down which the robber was supposed to have descended, easily convinced his silversmith of the falsity of the latter supposition, inasmuch as there was no soot on the hearth,—where, in truth, a fire was seldom made,—and no sign that any one had passed down the flue; and moreover that the chimney issued at a part of the roof which was almost inaccessible. At last, after two hours of close investigation, marked with that sagacity which distinguished the suspicious mind of Louis XI., it was clear to him, beyond all doubt, that no one had forced an entrance into the strong-room of his silversmith. No marks of violence were on the locks, nor on the iron coffers which contained the gold, silver, and jewels deposited as securities by wealthy debtors.

"If the robber opened this box," said the king, "why did he take nothing out of it but the jewels of the Duke of Bavaria? What reason had he for leaving that pearl necklace which lay beside them? A queer robber!"

At that remark the unhappy miser turned pale: he and the king looked at each other for a moment.

"Then, sire, what did that robber whom you have taken under your protection come to do here, and why did he prowl about at night?"

"If you have not guessed why, my crony, I order you to remain in ignorance. That is one of my secrets."

"Then the devil is in my house!" cried the miser, piteously.

In any other circumstances the king would have laughed at his silversmith's cry; but he had suddenly become thoughtful, and was casting on the Fleming those glances peculiar to men of talent and power which seem to penetrate the brain. Cornelius was frightened, thinking he had in some way offended his dangerous master.

"Devil or angel, I have him, the guilty man!" cried Louis XI. abruptly. "If you are robbed again to-night, I shall know to-morrow who did it. Make that old hag you call your sister come here," he added.

Cornelius almost hesitated to leave the king alone in the room with his hoards; but the bitter smile on Louis's withered lips determined him. Nevertheless he hurried back, followed by the old woman.

"Have you any flour?" demanded the king.

"Oh yes; we have laid in our stock for the winter," she answered.

"Well, go and fetch some," said the king.

"What do you want to do with our flour, sire?" she cried, not the least impressed by his royal majesty.

"Old fool!" said Cornelius, "go and execute the orders of our gracious master. Shall the king lack flour?"

"Our good flour!" she grumbled, as she went downstairs. "Ah! my flour!"

Then she returned, and said to the king:—

"Sire, is it only a royal notion to examine my flour?"

At last she reappeared, bearing one of those stout linen bags which, from time immemorial, have been used in Touraine to carry or bring, to and from market, nuts, fruits, or wheat. The bag was half full of flour. The housekeeper opened it and showed it to the king, on whom she cast the rapid, savage look with which old maids appear to squirt venom upon men.

"It costs six sous the 'septeree,'" she said.

"What does that matter?" said the king. "Spread it on the floor; but be careful to make an even layer of it—as if it had fallen like snow."

The old maid did not comprehend. This proposal astonished her as though the end of the world had come.

"My flour, sire! on the ground! But—"

Maitre Cornelius, who was beginning to understand, though vaguely, the intentions of the king, seized the bag and gently poured its contents on the floor. The old woman quivered, but she held out her hand for the empty bag, and when her brother gave it back to her she disappeared with a heavy sigh.

Cornelius then took a feather broom and gently smoothed the flour till it looked like a fall of snow, retreating step by step as he did so, followed by the king, who seemed much amused by the operation. When they reached the door Louis XI. said to his silversmith, "Are there two keys to the lock?"

"No, sire."

The king then examined the structure of the door, which was braced with large plates and bars of iron, all of which converged to a secret lock, the key of which was kept by Cornelius.

After examining everything, the king sent for Tristan, and ordered him to post several of his men for the night, and with the greatest secrecy, in the mulberry trees on the embankment and on the roofs of the adjoining houses, and to assemble at once the rest of his men and escort him back to Plessis, so as to give the idea in the town that he himself would not sup with Cornelius. Next, he told the miser to close his windows with the utmost care, that no single ray of light should escape from the house, and then he departed with much pomp for Plessis along the embankment; but there he secretly left his escort, and returned by a door in the ramparts to the house of the torconnier. All these precautions were so well taken that the people of Tours really thought the king had returned to Plessis, and would sup on the morrow with Cornelius.

Towards eight o'clock that evening, as the king was supping with his physician, Cornelius, and the captain of his guard, and holding much jovial converse, forgetting for the time being that he was ill and in danger of death, the deepest silence reigned without, and all passers, even the wariest robber, would have believed that the Malemaison was occupied as usual.

"I hope," said the king, laughing, "that my silversmith shall be robbed to-night, so that my curiosity may be satisfied. Therefore, messieurs, no one is to leave his chamber to-morrow morning without my order, under pain of grievous punishment."

Thereupon, all went to bed. The next morning, Louis XI. was

the first to leave his apartment, and he went at once to the door of the strong-room. He was not a little astonished to see, as he went along, the marks of a large foot along the stairways and corridors of the house. Carefully avoiding those precious footprints, he followed them to the door of the treasure-room, which he found locked without a sign of fracture or defacement. Then he studied the direction of the steps; but as they grew gradually fainter, they finally left not the slightest trace, and it was impossible for him to discover where the robber had fled.

"Ho, crony!" called out the king, "you have been finely robbed this time."

At these words the old Fleming hurried out of his chamber, visibly terrified. Louis XI. made him look at the foot-prints on the stairs and corridors, and while examining them himself for the second time, the king chanced to observe the miser's slippers and recognized the type of sole that was printed in flour on the corridors. He said not a word, and checked his laughter, remembering the innocent men who had been hanged for the crime. The miser now hurried to his treasure. Once in the room the king ordered him to make a new mark with his foot beside those already existing, and easily convinced him that the robber of his treasure was no other than himself.

"The pearl necklace is gone!" cried Cornelius. "There is sorcery in this. I never left my room."

"We'll know all about it now," said the king; the evident truthfulness of his silversmith making him still more thoughtful.

He immediately sent for the men he had stationed on the watch and asked:—

"What did you see during the night?"

"Oh, sire!" said the lieutenant, "an amazing sight! Your silversmith crept down the side of the wall like a cat; so lightly that he seemed to be a shadow."

"I!" exclaimed Cornelius; after that one word, he remained silent, and stood stock-still like a man who has lost the use of his limbs.

"Go away, all of you," said the king, addressing the archers, "and tell Messieurs Conyngham, Coyctier, Bridore, and also Tristan, to leave their rooms and come here to mine.—You have incurred the penalty of death," he said to Cornelius, who, happily, did not hear him. "You have ten murders on your conscience!"

Thereupon Louis XI. gave a silent laugh, and made a pause. Presently, remarking the strange pallor on the Fleming's face, he added:—

"You need not be uneasy; you are more valuable to bleed than to kill. You can get out of the claws of my justice by payment of a good round sum to my treasury, but if you don't build at least one chapel in honor of the Virgin, you are likely to find things hot for you throughout eternity."

"Twelve hundred and thirty, and eighty-seven thousand crowns, make thirteen hundred and seventeen thousand crowns," replied Cornelius mechanically, absorbed in his calculations. "Thirteen hundred and seventeen thousand crowns hidden somewhere!"

"He must have buried them in some hiding-place," muttered the king, beginning to think the sum royally magnificent. "That was the magnet that invariably brought him back to Tours. He felt his treasure."

Coyctier entered at this moment. Noticing the attitude of Maitre Cornelius, he watched him narrowly while the king related the adventure.

"Sire," replied the physician, "there is nothing supernatural in that. Your silversmith has the faculty of walking in his sleep. This is the third case I have seen of that singular malady. If you would give yourself the amusement of watching him at such times, you would see that old man stepping without danger at the very edge of the roof. I noticed in the two other cases I have already observed, a curious connection between the actions of that nocturnal existence and the interests and occupations of their daily life."

"Ah! Maitre Coyctier, you are a wise man."

"I am your physician," replied the other, insolently.

At this answer, Louis XI. made the gesture which was customary with him when a good idea was presented to his mind; he shoved up his cap with a hasty motion.

"At such times," continued Coyctier, "persons attend to their business while asleep. As this man is fond of hoarding, he has simply pursued his dearest habit. No doubt each of these attacks have come on after a day in which he has felt some fears about the safety of his treasure."

"Pasques-Dieu! and such treasure!" cried the king.

"Where is it?" asked Cornelius, who, by a singular provision of nature, heard the remarks of the king and his physician, while continuing himself almost torpid with thought and the shock of this singular misfortune.

"Ha!" cried Coyctier, bursting into a diabolical, coarse laugh, "somnambulists never remember on their waking what they have done when asleep."

"Leave us," said the king.

When Louis XI. was alone with his silversmith, he looked at him and chuckled coldly.

"Messire Hoogworst," he said, with a nod, "all treasures buried in France belong to the king."

"Yes, sire, all is yours; you are the absolute master of our lives and fortunes; but, up to this moment, you have only taken what you need."

"Listen to me, old crony; if I help you to recover this treasure, you can surely, and without fear, agree to divide it with me."

"No, sire, I will not divide it; I will give it all to you, at my death. But what scheme have you for finding it?"

"I shall watch you myself when you are taking your nocturnal tramps. You might fear any one but me."

"Ah, sire!" cried Cornelius, flinging himself at the king's feet, "you are the only man in the kingdom whom I would trust for such a service; and I will try to prove my gratitude for your goodness, by doing my utmost to promote the marriage of the Burgundian heiress with Monseigneur. She will bring you a noble treasure, not of money, but of lands, which will round out the glory of your crown."

"There, there, Dutchman, you are trying to hoodwink me," said the king, with frowning brows, "or else you have already done so."

"Sire! can you doubt my devotion? you, who are the only man I love!"

"All that is talk," returned the king, looking the other in the eyes. "You need not have waited till this moment to do me that service. You are selling me your influence—Pasques-Dieu! to me, Louis XI.! Are you the master, and am I your servant?"

"Ah, sire," said the old man, "I was waiting to surprise you agreeably with news of the arrangements I had made for you in Ghent; I was awaiting confirmation from Oosterlinck through that apprentice. What has become of that young man?"

"Enough!" said the king; "this is only one more blunder you have committed. I do not like persons to meddle in my affairs without my knowledge. Enough! leave me; I wish to reflect upon all this."

Maitre Cornelius found the agility of youth to run downstairs to the lower rooms where he was certain to find his sister.

"Ah! Jeanne, my dearest soul, a hoard is hidden in this house; I have put thirteen hundred thousand crowns and all the jewels somewhere. I, I, I am the robber!"

Jeanne Hoogworst rose from her stool and stood erect as if the seat she quitted were of red-hot iron. This shock was so violent for an old maid accustomed for years to reduce herself by voluntary fasts, that she trembled in every limb, and horrible pains were in her back. She turned pale by degrees, and her face,—the changes in which were difficult to decipher among its wrinkles,—became distorted while her brother explained to her the malady of which he was the victim, and the extraordinary situation in which he found himself.

"Louis XI. and I," he said in conclusion, "have just been lying to each other like two peddlers of coconuts. You understand, my girl, that if he follows me, he will get the secret of the hiding-place. The king alone can watch my wanderings at night. I don't feel sure that his conscience, near as he is to death, can resist thirteen hundred thousand crowns. We MUST be beforehand with him; we must find the hidden treasure and send it to Ghent, and you alone—"

Cornelius stopped suddenly, and seemed to be weighing the heart of the sovereign who had had thoughts of parricide at twenty-two years of age. When his judgment of Louis XI. was concluded, he rose abruptly like a man in haste to escape a pressing danger. At this instant, his sister, too feeble or too strong for such a crisis, fell stark; she was dead. Maitre Cornelius seized her, and shook her violently, crying out:

"You cannot die now. There is time enough later—Oh! it is all over. The old hag never could do anything at the right time."

He closed her eyes and laid her on the floor. Then the good and noble feelings which lay at the bottom of his soul came back to him, and, half forgetting his hidden treasure, he cried out mournfully:—

"Oh! my poor companion, have I lost you?—you who

understood me so well! Oh! you were my real treasure. There it lies, my treasure! With you, my peace of mind, my affections, all, are gone. If you had only known what good it would have done me to live two nights longer, you would have lived, solely to please me, my poor sister! Ah, Jeanne! thirteen hundred thousand crowns! Won't that wake you?—No, she is dead!"

Thereupon, he sat down, and said no more; but two great tears issued from his eyes and rolled down his hollow cheeks; then, with strange exclamations of grief, he locked up the room and returned to the king. Louis XI. was struck with the expression of sorrow on the moistened features of his old friend.

"What is the matter?" he asked.

"Ah! sire, misfortunes never come singly. My sister is dead. She precedes me there below," he said, pointing to the floor with a dreadful gesture.

"Enough!" cried Louis XI., who did not like to hear of death.

"I make you my heir. I care for nothing now. Here are my keys. Hang me, if that's your good pleasure. Take all, ransack the house; it is full of gold. I give up all to you—"

"Come, come, crony," replied Louis XI., who was partly touched by the sight of this strange suffering, "we shall find your treasure some fine night, and the sight of such riches will give you heart to live. I will come back in the course of this week—"

"As you please, sire."

At that answer the king, who had made a few steps toward the door of the chamber, turned round abruptly. The two men looked at each other with an expression that neither pen nor pencil can reproduce.

"Adieu, my crony," said Louis XI. at last in a curt voice, pushing up his cap.

"May God and the Virgin keep you in their good graces!" replied the silversmith humbly, conducting the king to the door of the house.

After so long a friendship, the two men found a barrier raised between them by suspicion and gold; though they had always been like one man on the two points of gold and suspicion. But they knew each other so well, they had so completely the habit, one may say, of each other, that the king could divine, from the tone in which Cornelius uttered the words, "As you please, sire," the repugnance that his visits would henceforth cause to the silversmith, just as the latter recognized a declaration of war in the "Adieu, my crony," of the king.

Thus Louis XI. and his torconnier parted much in doubt as to the conduct they ought in future to hold to each other. The monarch possessed the secret of the Fleming; but on the other hand, the latter could, by his connections, bring about one of the finest acquisitions that any king of France had ever made; namely, that of the domains of the house of Burgundy, which the sovereigns of Europe were then coveting. The marriage of the celebrated Marguerite depended on the people of Ghent and the Flemings who surrounded her. The gold and the influence of Cornelius could powerfully support the negotiations now begun by Desquerdes, the general to whom Louis XI. had given the command of the army encamped on the frontiers of Belgium. These two master-foxes were, therefore, like two duellists, whose arms are paralyzed by chance.

So, whether it were that from that day the king's health failed and went from bad to worse, or that Cornelius did assist in bringing into France Marguerite of Burgundy—who arrived at Ambroise in July, 1438, to marry the Dauphin to whom she was betrothed in the chapel of the castle—certain it is that the king took no steps in the matter of the hidden treasure; he levied no tribute from his silversmith, and the pair remained in the cautious condition of an armed friendship. Happily for Cornelius a rumor was spread about Tours that his sister was the actual robber, and that she had been secretly put to death by Tristan. Otherwise, if the true history had been known, the whole town would have risen as one man to destroy the Malemaison before the king could have taken measures to protect it.

But, although these historical conjectures have some foundation so far as the inaction of Louis XI. is concerned, it is not so as regards Cornelius Hoogworst. There was no inaction there. The silversmith spent the first days which succeeded that fatal night in ceaseless occupation. Like carnivorous animals confined in cages, he went and came, smelling for gold in every corner of his house; he studied the cracks and crevices, he sounded the walls, he besought the trees of the garden, the foundations of the house, the roofs of the turrets, the earth and the heavens, to give him back his treasure. Often he stood motionless for hours, casting his eyes on all sides, plunging them into the void. Striving for the miracles of ecstasy and the powers of sorcery, he tried to see his riches through space and obstacles. He was constantly absorbed in one overwhelming thought, consumed with a single desire that burned his entrails, gnawed more cruelly still by the ever-increasing agony of the duel he was fighting with himself since his passion for gold had turned to his own injury,—a species of uncompleted suicide which kept him at once in the miseries of life and in those of death.

Never was a Vice more punished by itself. A miser, locked by accident into the subterranean strong-room that contains his treasures, has, like Sardanapalus, the happiness of dying in the midst of his wealth. But Cornelius, the robber and the robbed, knowing the secret of neither the one nor the other, possessed and did not possess his treasure,—a novel, fantastic, but continually terrible torture. Sometimes, becoming forgetful, he would leave the little gratings of his door wide open, and then the passers in the street could see that already wizened man, planted on his two legs in the midst of his untilled garden, absolutely motionless, and casting on those who watched him a fixed gaze, the insupportable light of which froze them with terror. If, by chance, he walked through the streets of Tours, he seemed like a stranger in them; he knew not where he was, nor whether the sun or the moon were shining. Often he would ask his way of those who passed him, believing that he was still in Ghent, and seeming to be in search of something lost.

The most perennial and the best materialized of human ideas, the idea by which man reproduces himself by creating outside of himself the fictitious being called Property, that mental demon, drove its steel claws perpetually into his heart. Then, in the midst of this torture, Fear arose, with all its accompanying sentiments. Two men had his secret, the secret he did not know himself. Louis XI. or Coyctier could post men to watch him during his sleep and discover the unknown gulf into which he had cast his riches,— those riches he had watered with the blood of so many innocent men. And then, beside his fear, arose Remorse.

In order to prevent during his lifetime the abduction of his hidden treasure, he took the most cruel precautions against sleep; besides which, his commercial relations put him in the way of obtaining powerful anti-narcotics. His struggles to keep awake were awful—alone with night, silence, Remorse, and Fear, with all the thoughts that man, instinctively perhaps, has best embodied— obedient thus to a moral truth as yet devoid of actual proof.

At last this man so powerful, this heart so hardened by political and commercial life, this genius, obscure in history, succumbed to the horrors of the torture he had himself created. Maddened by certain thoughts more agonizing than those he had as yet resisted, he cut his throat with a razor.

This death coincided, almost, with that of Louis XI. Nothing then restrained the populace, and Malemaison, that Evil House, was pillaged. A tradition exists among the older inhabitants of Touraine that a contractor of public works, named Bohier, found the miser's treasure and used it in the construction of Chenonceaux, that marvellous chateau which, in spite of the wealth of several kings and the taste of Diane de Poitiers and Catherine de' Medici for building, remains unfinished to the present day.

Happily for Marie de Sassenage, the Comte de Saint-Vallier died, as we know, in his embassy. The family did not become extinct. After the departure of the count, the countess gave birth to a son, whose career was famous in the history of France under the reign of Francois I. He was saved by his daughter, the celebrated Diane de Poitiers, the illegitimate great-granddaughter of Louis XI., who became the illegitimate wife, the beloved mistress of Henri II.—for bastardy and love were hereditary in that family of nobles.

THE END